The Night Human Hunter

The Hunter Trilogy

Book 1

B. Kristin McMichael

The Night Human Hunter
Copyright © 2017 by B. Kristin McMichael
www.bkristinmcmichael.com
All rights reserved.

LEXIA
·PRESS·
Lexia Press, LLC
P.O. Box 982
Worthington, OH 43085
www.lexiapress.com

ISBN-10: 1-941745-07-5
ISBN-13: 978-1-941745-07-6

Cover design: Jessica Allain
Editors: Kathie Middlemiss of Kat's Eye Editing
Melissa of There For You Editing
Ashton M. Brammer

CONTENTS

CHAPTER 1

Jaxton Kristian ducked behind the nearest steel beam on the high-rise construction site. His older sister, Jade—only older by eleven months—stood in the open, waiting. Her neon green hair, the color of the month, stood out in the darkening sky like a star too close to Earth. Their target was bound to find her where she waited. Jax leaned just slightly to get a better view of his sister. She was already on her phone, typing away, an obvious sign of boredom. Jax didn't mind the waiting part of a hunt, but Jade did. He didn't dare look toward the beam next to him where Rommy waited. She would be furious at Jade's lack of enthusiasm.

A loud shriek brought Jax's attention to the sky. A large bird was flying maybe two hundred yards to the east. Jax set down his rifle. It was heading directly to Jade, as they had planned, and he wasn't going to need to shoot it out of the sky … not that that would have been a problem. The night human was doing just what they wanted. Jax pulled out his pistol and waited in his hiding spot.

Jade finally tucked her phone into her pocket before bending down to slip two of the daggers out of the sheaths she had strapped onto her legs. As stand-offish as her appearance and attitude was, she liked to fight in close combat. Their teacher, Rommy, preferred a sword to keep her distance, but Jade liked to be able to see their eyes at all times.

In one swoop, the bird creature landed with a thump in front of Jade. Knowing where her brother was hiding, Jade positioned slightly to give Jax the best view of the situation since he was her back-up. He was always her back-up. Being only eleven months apart and in the same grade at school meant they were raised almost like twins. All their time together made them actually act like twins also, and the age difference never mattered. Jax had to learn quickly how to be on par with his older sister. Jade was ready for the fight, and Jax wasn't going to let her fail.

The ugly night human stood over six feet tall, with gray, ratted hair that hung down between her two enormous, white-tipped, black-feathered wings. It wasn't just her wings that made her stand out as not being human, but also the talons on her feet and her beak-like nose. The bird lady would never not be mistaken for what she really was: a blood-thirsty monster.

Lifting an arm out from beneath her ragged purple cape, the creature dropped something on the ground between Jade and herself.

"I got the message, hunter," the bird lady rasped. Even her voice didn't sound human.

Jade didn't glance down, but Jax did. He had seen it before, yet still had to look. It was the severed head Jade had left outside their nest. Jade was certain it would provoke the leader of the group out to fight, and sure enough, as the gold medallion that indicated her position swung around bird lady's neck, it had.

"Actually, I don't think you did get the message. You only brought me one head, and that was the one I had to dispatch myself," Jade replied. Normally Jade was a quiet girl that would prefer to hide in her own shadow, but once she was in hunter mode, she was completely different, with a confidence Jax would love to see in real life.

The feathered night human sneered at Jade.

"The treaty between the council and harpies dictates that you'll only ever keep a nest of three harpies. From our count, there are close to a dozen here now. You have broken the rules and thus forfeit your life."

Without waiting for a reply, Jade threw all five-foot-five of herself at a creature almost a foot taller than her. Jax smiled. He loved it when his sister was her real self. There was no fear in her eyes as she sliced her daggers across the surprised night human. The harpy had moved her arm to keep the cut from severing her own head. That was Jade's one chance to surprise her as the bird lady stepped back and started to calculate her own response. Jax had hoped it would work as they had talked about beforehand, but he knew better. This harpy would be harder to kill. She was their leader and stronger than the rest.

Jax dropped low to the ground, and army-crawled from the beam he was standing behind to a stack of construction supplies approximately ten feet in front of him. He would need a better position to take down the bird if Jade got stuck. He wouldn't want to miss his shot and hit his sister. Jax was hidden much better than Jade had been, as he was dressed all in black from his head to toe. Even with his black hair, the only visible part of him was his face, which he kept toward the ground while he crawled.

As he made it to the pile, he slowly moved to a kneeling position behind the lumber to see how much the fight had changed in the few moments it took to crawl. Surprisingly, not much. The harpy was still dripping blood as she circled away from Jade. Jade was slowly moving in step with the bird while keeping just out of the reach of the bird's clawed arms as she assessed the situation.

The girls continued to circle each other, but neither moved closer. The bird seemed to sense that Jade was more of a threat than she appeared. Jax could almost smile at that. Most people underestimated him and his sister, but being raised by one of the best night human hunters out there had its perks. Jax leveled his gun in front of him. Jade had a time limit because the rest of the team was hitting the nest soon to reduce the number of harpies. They had already picked a successor that was willing to keep to the rules. Without the leader at the nest, the team would have no trouble eliminating the rest of the harpies.

Jax had the shot and waited for his sister's approval before a hand came up beside him and pulled it down.

'This is her fight,' Rommy mouthed to him. They were too close to speak now as the bird would know their position if they did.

Jax glared at Rommy. Jade was his sister and the only family he cared about. There was no way he was going to let her be skewered by a bird to prove that she wasn't ready to be a full-time hunter. Rommy and he both knew Jade was more than ready to join the hunters as a full-fledged member, but there was always the possibility for even the best hunter to be taken down by an unpredictable night human ... especially one that knew it was her death if she lost.

Moving to raise his gun again, Rommy grabbed his wrist hard and held it down.

'We don't interrupt her or she fails.'

Who cared about failing? Jax almost wanted to pretend he couldn't lip read. He already knew what Rommy was telling him, but he'd rather pretend he didn't. The hunters had their outdated rules and rituals, like having to hunt the head of a clan to join as a full hunter, but Jax really didn't care. Which was more important, his sister's life or advancing as a full hunter? Jade would be mad at him for weeks if he took down the bird, mainly because then his night human kills on missions would outnumber hers, but he still didn't care about any of that. None of that mattered to him. Hunters were human, and he wasn't about to lose his sister over a stupid test.

Rommy twisted his wrist and the pain bit into his arm as the bones were smashed together. It hurt, but his pain tolerance was considerable for only being a normal human. Hunters had to deal with pain all the time, and he had been more than accustomed it with Rommy training him. She glared at him as she squeezed the bones closer together. He knew that face all too well. Rommy wasn't going to let him take the shot, probably not even if Jade's life depended on it.

Jax glared at the lady holding him back. There was little love between them. He was sure she was going to let the test go, but he was also sure that he wasn't going to let Jade die doing it. It was a battle of wills as they glared at each other.

His arm ached, but he wasn't about to start taking orders from the older hunter. Pulling hard at both his hand and Rommy's hand on him, he propped up his gun on the stack of wood as his wrist crunched. She wasn't holding back tonight. Oh well, it wasn't the first time Rommy had broken a bone on him, and it would heal rapidly. It always did. He wasn't a full-fledged hunter, but he did heal abnormally fast for a regular human. It would be good as new in a few days.

Jax watched the fight between his sister and the bird. Neither had thrown a blow yet, but it was coming. The bird circled again, and Jax caught the slight smile on her face. This wasn't good. Jax had seen the harpy in action when they'd been tailing her clan. Picking up on personality ticks was a pastime of Jax's that he did when they spent so much time watching someone. That smile told him that it wasn't safe for Jade. Jax centered his aim. He had the bird in his sights. Jade was taking too long, and he needed to end it. Her chances of winning were getting smaller as each moment passed, and he couldn't risk her life on this one test. As Jade's teacher and mentor, Rommy should have been the one to step in and stop it, but she obviously wasn't going to. Jax would take it upon himself to end this mission successfully before anything happened to Jade.

Jax pulled the trigger, and the bird looked directly at him with a smile. *Who smiles when they're about to die?* Someone who was prepared. The bird took Jade quicker than humanly possible and shifted her directly into the line of the bullet. It hit straight on as it smashed through her head and blood splattered everywhere around them. Hunters could heal from most wounds, but like a night human, a head shot was fatal. Stunned for only moments, everything rushed at him at once. Jax felt his world crumble around him. His life was over. Jade was the only one who mattered, and his bullet just went through her. He had killed his sister.

Jax didn't feel it as the claws ripped into him only moments after his sister's death. Rommy was just as surprised as she turned to join the fight, but didn't have time. That's how well planned everything was happening around Jax. She was a legend in the hunter world, and this had caught *her* off guard. Jax would say she was stunned from Jade dying, but that wasn't true. Rommy didn't care either way. These birds were prepared, and as he took his last breath he could see that the whole dozen harpies had come out to play with them, even the traitor who had offered to rule the nest if the hunters killed off their leader. They had been double-crossed, but they should have expected that from night humans. They were never to be trusted. Jax let his eyes fall closed with the image of his dead sister in front of him. Even if he could move, he didn't have any fight left in him. The world dimmed.

Jax reopened his eyes to see he was still standing behind the construction materials, his broken wrist hanging at his side while the other hand was still aiming at the harpy circling his sister. He didn't have time to sit and contemplate the visions he had just seen. It had happened again. He knew what it meant. The first time a vision came to him, he'd been lucky. Jade didn't need his help, and he could sit stupefied since he had seen the future, and then watching it play out exactly as he had seen. The second time it happened, he acted to change the future, and he could. He hadn't told Rommy about his handy new skill yet, but Jade knew. It wasn't the kind of thing he could keep from her.

Jax didn't hesitate as he stood up, revealing himself from his hiding spot. Rommy was likely too caught off guard to stop him.

"WC," Jax yelled, and Jade didn't miss a beat as she ducked under the harpy lady's outstretched arms and dove off the side of the building behind her the opposite direction from Jax. That was their code word that they were done. Jax made the call today, but Jade could also. They had complete trust in each other, but that was to be expected since they were raised together, learning everything at the same time.

Jax moved the opposite direction from Jade as planned and quickly took to the unfinished staircase. While momentarily surprised, Rommy was close behind him, keeping pace. He didn't have time to check on Jade, but he hoped she would also take cover. They needed to get to their meet-up point, and fast, before calling the other hunters. There could be a trap waiting for them, also.

Taking the stairs two at a time Jax passed by several floors, hoping he wouldn't see the rest of the nest. As each floor was empty, he had to hope they were all hiding in the skies and not chasing Jade. In reality, she was more of a target than he was as she did the actual killing of the harpy they used to drag out the leader. Nearing the last level, he paused. Their car was parked near the building, but at the same time, the driver's seat faced the open lot. It would be easy for a harpy to swoop down and take him before he could get inside, and it was possible—with the number he had seen—that there was at least half a dozen following him and half a dozen following Jade.

Jax didn't check with Rommy as he flattened himself against the building, pistol drawn, while he hurried to the car. Rommy took his cue and followed. She might like to call the shots, but when Jax was moving, she wasn't about to stop to ask questions. At least she trusted Jax and Jade that much, or it might have been her sixth sense. Rommy had gotten out of more life-threatening situations than any other hunter, creating quite a name for herself. Jax made it to the passenger side and slid in to climb across to the driver's side. Rommy followed, and Jax started up the car without looking to the skies like Rommy was. He knew what she was going to see.

"They're here," she commented, surprised by what she

saw now that she had time to look around.

"And we're going to go pick up Jade now. Screw the test, we were betrayed," Jax told her, peeling out of their parking spot with just one hand on the wheel. Luckily that car was an automatic or there would be a lot of pain to get home.

He could feel the bones crunching as they tried to realign correctly in his broken wrist. Healing was one of the hunter perks he had, but he'd have rather not be dealing with it at the moment. He'd thank Rommy for it, but she'd probably just break it again for him giving her sass.

"You have a meet-up point?" Rommy asked.

"Always."

Jax didn't slow down as he rounded the half-built building. As expected, on the other side several harpies had already landed on the ground. Jade was quicker, but easier to follow as she had left off the side of the building and scaled to the ground. She was now backed against the building as the harpies prevented her from going toward the door to the inside. The harpies knew that they couldn't fight as well in close quarters. Their size and wings got in the way indoors. In fact, they lived in a cave because of the need for space. If Jade made it into the building, they wouldn't have a chance to kill her. Jax didn't slow down as he plowed into the harpies and stopped only inches from his sister. Rommy already had the door open, and Jade slid inside.

Jax clenched his teeth as he used his broken arm to throw the car into reverse. He turned the wheel to back over the harpies he had already run over and who were still lying on the ground. A car wouldn't kill a night human, but like bowling pins, he could knock them down so they would have to get back up before coming after him. He didn't wait to see if the car did any permanent damage to the downed monsters as he peeled out of the dirt lot and found the waiting paved road.

It wasn't going to be an easy out as he hoped. There were too many of them, and there were more than one still standing when he went harpy bowling with his car. With a loud thunk, a harpy landed on the roof of the car.

"I'd normally take care of that myself, but since you had to go and break my wrist, the bird is all yours," Jax said as he continued to drive. He had no doubt that between his sister and mother, one harpy wasn't going to be a problem.

"Really, Mom?" Jade complained from the backseat as she was pulling out a gun to shoot at the trailing harpies. "Did you have to go and injure Jax when it was very possible we'd still need him? Couldn't you wait until we got home?" Jade turned around to see how many weapons she needed to pull out.

"How was I supposed to know they were going to betray us?" Rommy asked in reply. She rolled down her window to take care of the one on the roof of the car that was trying to dig a hole in the metal over their heads. The harpy was doing a pretty good job for not having anything but its claws.

"Because they're night humans, duh," Jade replied. "Isn't that the first lesson of hunting? Never trust a night human?" Jade's snarkiness fell on deaf ears since Rommy was already hanging out the window, slicing at the night human taking the free ride. Jade rolled her eyes at her brother and slammed the back of her gun into the car rear window, giving herself a bigger hole to shoot from.

"Glad I took the older car now, aren't you?" Jax yelled to his sister. His words made her roll her eyes again as she leveled the gun to shoot at any bird lady that got too close.

Jax took a sharp turn, which forced the night human on the top to swing closer to Rommy. With the bird near enough, she made short work of the harpy and pulled herself back into the car. Jax didn't turn to look and see if his mother was alright. It didn't matter how fast he drove or what sharp corners he took, she'd be fine. Rommy barely ever returned home with anything more than a scratch on her. Jax often wondered if she really was human.

Jade let out a warning shot to a bird that was getting too

close. Night humans rarely fought with guns, so it was enough to make them stay back.

"We'll have to get the others and go back at dawn," Rommy commented as she wiped off her blade so that it shined in the moonlight coming through the trees.

Jax nodded. Sometimes, especially while a broken bone was healing, he wished he had been born into another life. Being a teen was hard enough, but throw in being the child of a legendary hunter and life was just plain old exhausting. He should have been used to it, but he wasn't. It was just another Friday night in the Kristian household that mirrored everything he had grown up with. Saturday morning would be spent killing off monsters that were hurting humans. It would be nice if hunter life had time to take a break, but his mother was right—they needed to finish off the nest and move on to their next assignment. Life never slowed down for hunters.

After the harpies, Rommy found Jade a sure thing to pass her hunters test. Jax didn't need to help this time, but he had to come along as he was assigned as her permanent backup. He actually had been partnered with her since they started hunting without an adult. In the history of their hunts, this had to be one of the dullest he'd ever been on. Considering he'd been hunting his entire life, he had a lot to compare it to. Jade didn't need help to get rid of her night human target, and easy didn't even come close to describing the hunt. Jax couldn't think of any word that would prove what a waste of time it was. It was more than hard to believe the night human was actually even a night human.

Night humans were creatures who lived on blood. More accurately, they were humans that lived on blood and in exchange could do extraordinary things. Once, Jax had seen a night human spew acid from their insides that melted a car, and another that walked through a wall. Their abilities ranged based on what they were, and all night humans could be classified into a family. Most of the time night humans kept to themselves and didn't hurt the rest of the people, but some didn't like the rules that forbid them from killing regular old day humans. That's when the hunters were called in.

Hunters were normal humans and thankfully didn't need blood to survive. Jax couldn't stand to watch night humans feed. He was also thankful that being a hunter had many perks. Hunters were born into their lives, and normal day humans knew nothing about them. In fact, most normal day humans didn't know the night human world existed. Jax knew and appreciated the gifts he was given. He was stronger, quicker, and healed faster than a normal human. He needed less sleep, had better sight, and a much better memory. All of that came without the need for blood, and it made it possible for day humans to hunt the bad night humans. And that is how they were raised—to kill night humans. From a young age, they were trained for hours every day on how to fight and what all the night humans were capable of. They were prepared for a life of fighting and danger, and were given no choice how to live. All hunters were expected to hunt, Jax and Jade were no exception, but he'd hardly call what Jade did to pass her exam hunting.

Jade was easily able to pass and become a full-fledged hunter. It wasn't because she was a year older that Jax didn't take the test. He was never going to be allowed to test. The hunter gene that made them what they were was passed down the female lineage. He was only a lowly male that could never continue the line of protectors the day humans needed. He was a second class citizen in the hunter world. Yes, Jax was happy for his older sister, but her passing that one exam changed everything.

As he sat at their latest hunt … well, as he sat as lookout

and Jade sat distracted on her phone, Jax realized just what his life was going to be like. Jax would have to keep hunting and doing everything they were taught, and Jade would show up to boss him around. He had seen the hunter men in the groups at times, and none of them seemed happy. It was actually more common for a hunter to not have a husband than have one. Jade and Jax had never met their dad, and their mother refused to tell them who he was. Now Jax could see why the men didn't stick around, as he was always left to keep his eyes on the house while she was busy with friends. It was a far cry from the partnership they had shared only weeks before.

"Anything more?" Jade asked from the backseat of the car where she was lounging. She didn't even come to the front seat. From the looks of her, you couldn't tell she was on a mission.

Jax didn't feel like answering. She could sit up and look around if she wanted to know more. She was just lazy. Now that she was a full member in the hunter group, it seemed like she was growing more and more lazy—and bossy at that. Hunting used to be fun and a time to get away from their mother—something they could do together—but not so much in the past couple weeks since her advancement. Jax had gone on three hunts with her, and they were all exactly alike; Jade acting like the Queen of Sheba, and Jax getting the job done because someone needed to save those unsuspecting day humans.

Tucking his hands into his pockets, he just stared ahead. The car was off, but it wasn't cold. They hadn't been there long enough that if someone stopped by, they would know they had just parked. He kept his hands tucked away because he didn't want to grip the steering wheel as hard as he would when she was grating on his nerves. The car didn't deserve to be beat up because Jade needed an attitude adjustment. And she needed one majorly.

The worst part of it all was she didn't seem to notice

anything had changed. Jade had been his best friend growing up, and they had done everything together. They were all each other had as they moved constantly and their mother was anything but motherly, but now it wasn't like that. She seemed to have all sorts of new friends. All the full-fledged hunters were friends with each other, but not with the lower hunters in the family. She had ditched him the first time someone called her their new friend. It wasn't the two of them against the world anymore. It was Jade off playing with her new hunter friends, and Jax having to pick up the slack for her new lazy ways.

"If they aren't coming out tonight, then let's head over to the meeting early," Jade suggested, finally sitting up and flicking her deep purple hair out of her face.

Jax wanted to argue and explain that it had been over a week since they last saw their latest night humans. Those night humans would have to come out to feed, and that would be in the next day or so. Night humans could not go forever without food. Jax and Jade were better off waiting now to catch them than to go to a meeting they really didn't need to attend. In fact, they had yet to go to one they really needed to. Anything they missed, their mother would tell them anyways. Jade should have known this much.

"Is that an order?" Jax asked, anger lacing his tone even if he didn't want to sound that way.

Jade stared at him from the backseat for a long moment like she was considering her options. Maybe the old Jade was going to come out. Eventually, she nodded and, looking back at her phone, texted away to someone. Nope, the new Jade was still sticking around.

Jax ground his teeth as he started up the car. In the corner of the window in the front of the house he was watching, Jax saw the curtain flicker a little. Someone was waiting for them to leave, he was certain of it. He wanted to tell Jade, but he knew what she would say. It wasn't an illusion, but he was sure Jade would make it seem like it had been. She had already made up her mind, and he didn't get a say. He used to get a say. They had made really good partners before. That was gone now.

"Their deaths are on your head," Jax told her as he put the car in drive and peeled out of the across-the-street driveway. Jax felt sorry for all those day humans they could see in their lit windows as they drove away. The night human wouldn't go far to feed, and they were all in the path.

Those leeches would be out roaming tonight, and there wouldn't be a hunter around to stop them. Some innocent day human was going to be their meal, and the hunters would be left with a cold trail to try to follow. They were smart enough to not stick around, and it might take weeks or longer to find where they moved to. Jax loved the chase and the hunt, but he hated to lose them. Night humans lived on human blood. They roamed the streets and sucked innocent victims dry daily. He was thrilled to have the training to stop them. There were good night humans that didn't kill and drank donated blood from blood banks, but he didn't worry about them. There were plenty of others that preferred to have a warm tasty meal, and even more of them that simply liked to drain the day humans dry. Jax was willing to off those leeches, just like the ones that would be out roaming the second they were out of sight. He hated to have to drive away. Jade used to hate losing another human life also, but she didn't seem to mind now.

Jax didn't say a word to his sister as they drove to the next town over where the meeting was taking place. He was more than a little mad at her, and he didn't have to speak as she was sure to be too busy to talk back anyway. It wasn't like she noticed the silence or even tried to care that someone, or multiple someone's, would be dying tonight. Her new friends needed her time. There was all sorts of girlie gossip they needed to catch up on.

To some extent he understood. Jade had been shy her whole life and never made friends in all the schools they had attended. Being a hunter was the only thing that was real for her, and to finally have friends that were also hunters made it more appealing. There were several girls her age who were inducted as full-fledged hunters in the past six months. He understood, but that didn't mean he approved of her new attitude. She needed to find a balance between new friends and keeping humans safe from bloodsuckers. Sure, he was the younger brother, and that was the biggest reason why she was in charge, but he was also the more responsible of the two. Heck, in two months he would be eighteen and a legal adult, but he didn't need that title to understand responsibility.

Driving in silence, Jax stole a few glances back at Jade. She was still busy typing on her phone and smiling, which was just about enough to melt his anger. Jade rarely smiled when talking to people. The pressure and expectations that went with being the great Rommy's daughter were rough on her. Then all the moving took its toll. Jax had conflicted feelings. He was still angry at her for losing their hunt because of a bad choice, but he was also genuinely happy for her.

Jax parked on the street in front of the house they were meeting at since the driveway was already full. They didn't seem to be the only ones who headed over early.

Jade hopped out of the car without a look back. That part was hard to get used to. She seemed to not even care about him anymore. When she ran up the stairs and into the house, Jax slowly followed behind her. There was no reason for him to go running anywhere. As a guy, he wasn't going to be allowed past the front room. No super secrets for him.

Entering the room, Jax looked around. Three of the husbands were already sitting down and talking, and two younger boys were sitting together also. There weren't any hunters his age around. Well, one of the husbands was his age, but Jax being single with absolutely no plans to marry put them on two different levels, even if the guy was only two years older than him.

Sitting near the door, Jax pulled out his own phone. There wouldn't be anything new on it. He didn't have many friends himself, but the ones he did have were great. And he could overlook the fact that one of his newest friends was a night human. But she was the good kind. He hadn't spoken to her or her boyfriend in months, but he was looking forward to her boyfriend getting back to his singing career. He might have promised Jax to do one of the songs that Jax had written. They were still night humans and connected to the night human world, but it was the first chance in Jax's life to do something that wasn't really night human-ish—by having a song recorded for a real album that thousands of people would hear.

More female hunters came into the room and passed through the door. Most were talking together or listening in on whatever was being talked about. Not a single one glanced at the males all sitting around and waiting. Soon enough, Jax's own mother came into the room, but she didn't just pass by.

"Did you catch if they are still there?" Rommy asked as she stopped in front of Jax, towering over him where he sat. Jax hated to have to bend back so far to look up at her, but it wasn't a choice.

"I think they are, but like I told Jade, they will use our absence to hunt, and we'll have to track them again. We've been there long enough; they had to know. Otherwise, they would have come out," Jax replied. He was one of the few people that didn't fear talking to his mother. Yes, she had a temper and wasn't afraid to break a bone or two—even in her own son—but that was it. She wasn't going to kill him.

"And why didn't you convince her to stay then? Why the heck are you guys here?" Rommy asked the same question he had asked himself. Rommy was not one for leaving a hunt unfinished. That might have been one trait Jax actually inherited from her, but that was it.

"I don't get a say, remember, Mother?" Jax replied, finally standing up as his anger grew. He wasn't going to argue with her towering above him. Rommy expected him to keep going as if things were normal when things were anything but. Now he stood taller than his mother. Jax didn't want to gloat or feel power over her, but just wanted the heck out of the depressing hunter house.

Rommy raised an eyebrow at Jax. If he stayed long enough, it meant a broken rib or possibly finger, even in front of everyone. Rommy didn't care if people saw her hurt her own kids. They were hers to punish as she saw fit. Jax knew that firsthand as he grew up and noticed that no one would stop her.

"A couple weeks ago, Jade would have listened to me, but you had to go and change all of that. I'll see you at home."

Not waiting around to see what Rommy had to say, Jax stormed out of the hunter's meeting house. He was sure to be punished for speaking to her like that once she got home from the meeting, but there was no way she would leave early to do that. Punishing her kid came below meetings, while the hunt would always come before everything. He had a few hours until she returned back to the crappy, rundown place they were renting now, so he was free from pain for a bit. Jax really didn't want to go back to the depressing shamble that they were calling home.

Without anywhere else to go, Jax headed back to the house where the night humans had been. They wouldn't be there; he was sure. He could at least see if there was a fresh trail to follow. They had to be long gone, but he'd get a head start on tracking them … again. It wasn't like they were easy to track the first time, but Jade didn't care. She didn't do much of that either, now. Maybe if they had blonde ponytails and carried cell phones, Jade would care a bit at least.

Unfortunately, he didn't make it to the night humans' house, just their street before an ambulance blocked the way.

Jax considered going around to the other side of the block to get closer to the place, but instead pulled off to the side and jumped out of his car.

"Stay behind the tape," an officer directed people who were starting to gather at the scene of an apparent crime.

Jax turned and walked behind the crowd, over to where the ambulance was parked. With no one looking, he ducked under the tape and slid closer to the vehicle to stay in the shadows. Silently, Jax made his way over to the open back doors and paused when he heard two people talking. Their voices were clear enough to listen in.

"I have no idea what kind of animal got into their house, but there isn't a single person left alive in there." The voice was soft, but masculine. It sounded scared.

Jax looked at the house the vehicle was parked in front of. The door was wide open, and there was enough blood on the porch that he didn't need to view the inside to know the man talking was telling the truth. More than likely the night humans had gone on a feeding frenzy. They probably shredded the defenseless day humans to pieces. They wouldn't have even seen it coming until they were all dead. It wasn't the first time Jax had viewed how these particular monsters fed. He had to see it to track them. It wasn't a good sight, and he felt bad for the unprepared man that had seen it.

"How many did they find?" a second voice asked. Again it was male, but in much better control of his emotions.

"Four. Two adults and two kids," the first voice replied. "It was horrible. The kids were ripped apart, like, their limbs torn from them." It sounded as if the first man was about to start crying.

"Don't worry. The people doing this will be caught," the second voice told him.

"People?" the first voice asked.

"Now you're going to forget everything you saw and will see as you clean up the place. The animal that attacked these people was caught and taken care of by animal control.

There is no more need to worry."

"No more need to worry," the first voice repeated in a dull voice, all emotion drained from it.

Jax slid to be able to view the people talking through the crack. Something was going on, and he needed to know what it was. He could tell someone was using a persuasion or a spell, but he wasn't sure who. Night human tricks didn't work on him, but they weren't the only ones who knew spells like that. Jax peered through the crack and only saw one person, an EMT who was preparing to stand and go to work cleaning up the mess that just had him terrified. He moved robotically away from the ambulance. There wasn't a second person.

Jax turned to sneak back to his car. He didn't need to see more or find out who the person was that was with the man. No matter if he was a night or day human, Jax didn't need him. He needed to find the vicious night humans that had feasted on the family in the house before him. The night humans he had been tracking had to be the one responsible for everything, and he hadn't been there to stop it. It would be too much of a mess with all the people already going in and out of the house to track the monsters from it, and he'd have to start all over. He doubted Jade would help. Part of Jax wanted to take a picture and send it to her, but for now, he just wanted to leave. It was their fault these people were dead, Jade and his. If they had done their job, they would have been safe.

"Not going to stick around and see if the charm works?" someone asked Jax from behind.

Jax turned slowly, inching the blade that was strapped to his wrist down into his hand.

The man standing before him was dressed all in black, just like Jax dressed when he was hunting. His bright blue eyes seemed amused as he observed. He held up his hands in the surrender position, tossing his blond bangs out of his eyes.

"Whoa, cowboy. You can just keep those to yourself." He pointed to Jax's hands. "You and I do the same job."

Not being one to take advice from a night human, Jax kept the blade in his hand. He wasn't about to trust a stranger, never mind one that he was pretty sure was a night human. Jax had a gift of being able to tell who night humans were by shaking their hands, but his talent was getting stronger now. Some he was able to tell by just looking at them. This guy had the whole night human feeling around him. Jax kept his eyes trained on him as he backed up.

"You think if I wanted to fight, I'd talk first? Really, kid?"

Now Jax was certain. The guy in front of him looked like he wasn't much older than him. There was no way Jax was a "kid" to him unless he was older than he appeared. He had to be a night human, but who or what kind was more the mystery. Yes, Jax was going to keep his guard up. He'd be stupid to not do so.

"I just wanted to let you know that I caught the guys in the act. I was able to take out the whole hive, and you don't need to keep looking for them. Tell the hunters this case is closed."

"The whole hive?" Jax asked. He was just one man. Jade and Jax had hoped to take out the ones that were feeding, but not the whole hive. Heck, they didn't know where the whole hive was at this point.

"Yes. Thanks to you and your sister, I was able to track you here and finish it off. You leaving gave me the perfect opportunity to strike. They thought it was only you two and didn't know I was even there."

So he got rid of all of them, yet that didn't add up.

"And then why is there a family dead?"

The man glanced back to the house, not afraid to take his eyes off Jax. The blue-eyed stranger looked back at Jax and shrugged.

"Day humans aren't my problem. One got loose when I

was killing the hive, and by the time I caught him, he was here trying to get enough blood to fight me. He lost. Don't worry about that."

Jax was already close enough to the back of the ambulance to walk away without worrying about being attacked, but something made him stay. He stared at the man in front of him. He wasn't sure what kind of night human the man was, though he knew a lot of different kinds. Jax was sure the man was one, but he just didn't seem as monstrous as they normally were. Yes, Jax had a night human friend, and she was as far from monster as they came, but this man was different. He didn't feel like a monster, but everything about him said "dangerous, stay away."

"Well, it was nice meeting you, Jaxton Kristian, but I need to get on my way." The man made an elaborate bow to him.

"You know who I am?"

"Yes, and your father sends his regards," the man replied, giving Jax a wink.

"My father?" Now Jax was curious. A night human that knew his name and his father was more than an oddity, and something Jax wanted to know more about.

"Check the trash when you get home, and you might get an answer." That was all the man said before he disappeared from view.

Jax didn't look over his shoulder or drive down the block to see the empty house that he had been watching all week. For some reason, he trusted that the man had killed off the night humans they were hunting. For now, Jax needed to go home and see what was in the trash before his mother or sister came back. For the first time in his life, someone had mentioned his father. He had spent years searching each house they lived in, and his mother's stuff secretly, but there was nothing to be found. Jax didn't even know his father's initials let alone his name, and he knew Kristian was his mother's name. He always wanted to know more, and he was possibly getting that chance—if he could trust the mysterious night human.

Jax didn't stop to get the mail as he barreled into the house. He was going to have to deal with his mother for how he talked to her, so he might as well add not getting the mail to the list of things he was going to get yelled at for. And he wasn't going to do any other boring chore she expected of him, either. He was done with that. He was already made servant to his sister on hunts; he wasn't going to live like that at home. In fact, it was about time he found a place. The hunter's association paid him for his work. It wasn't much, but if he found a roommate or two, he could live on his own. He needed to get away from his family.

Jax pushed into the broken-down kitchen where the only trash can in the whole house was. There were leftovers from the past week in there, so it wasn't going to be fun digging through. He had to just hope the leech wasn't pulling his leg and there really was something in the trash as he began to dig through it. Jax held his breath and pushed away the week-old Chinese and pepperoni pizza mix that was the trash. Without knowing what he was searching for, he had to look at each item as he dug through the mess. Papers, newspapers, boxes, wrappers, everything was in the trash. Each new piece of slime he touched made him cringe, but he kept digging. It took a few minutes to go far enough into the mess to find a sealed envelope.

The standard-sized envelope was addressed to both him and his mother, and postmarked from a week ago. His mother had never mentioned it, and it wasn't opened. Maybe she didn't know what was inside. Jax read the return address, a law firm in New Orleans. That was states away from where they were, and as far as he knew they didn't know anyone there. Jax had been there once when he went with another hunter, and his mother chewed that hunter out so much that she didn't return to help Jax train anymore after that. He never knew what it was about, and he didn't have a choice. He wasn't allowed to ask questions. The great hunter Rommy told you what she wanted you to know, and she didn't want him to know something. No one was going to go against her, and he was just a kid. He let it go. Now it was clear, based on the fact that she threw the unopened envelope away, that there was something in New Orleans.

Wiping off the little bit of food on the corner of the envelope—it had been saved from most of the mess because it was between papers in the trash—he slid his finger under the seal. He was pretty sure no one knew where they were right now. They hadn't been renting the crap hole they were in for that long. They traveled all the time and were in a new city practically every month, yet the envelope was addressed to him. Someone knew. The location of the envelope being in the trash, hidden from view, made it seem that his mother didn't want him to discover it.

Jax pulled the paper from inside the envelope and stared in shock. It was a check addressed to him for more money than he was sure his mother made in six months working for the hunters. The check was written to him, and in the note space at the bottom, it said *payment 167*. Jax didn't need to do the math to know his family didn't have that kind of money anywhere and besides, his mother had thrown the check away without opening it. In fact, as he looked closer, there was nothing on the outside to indicate that it was a check at all. How did his mother know to throw it away? Was it an accident?

Jax shook his head. His mother never did anything by accident, and it was clearly more than just a coincidence that his mother freaked out about him going to New Orleans, where the check originated from. But what did it mean? Who was sending them money— lots of money at that? And why didn't his mother cash it? It would be much easier, and they wouldn't have to live in the crappiest places they could afford if they had the kind of money the check was offering. And if she'd cashed one hundred of the checks already, they could even stay in nice hotels everywhere they went. And Jax could drive a nice car. He really wanted one that he didn't have to work on every weekend just to keep running.

Things weren't adding up. Jax didn't understand why the check was in his name, let alone who was sending it. Jax glanced at the outside of the envelope. The only clue he had to go on was an address for a law firm named "Lawrence and Sons". They would know who was sending the money and what it meant.

Looking at the clock, Jax understood he had little time to decide what to do. He had two options if he wanted answers. He could wait around and ask his mother, and she was bound to be in a bad mood from earlier. She probably was planning to punish him for speaking out of place earlier, so it was likely an answer wasn't in the cards. Or he could take a road trip. He hadn't been paid enough money from the hunters to cover gas and hotels for a trip that far away, but the check in his hand would make it possible for him to investigate what it all meant. He was quite likely to get more answers from a stranger than his mother.

Jax grabbed the check and ran upstairs to his room. There wasn't much to pack; in reality, he didn't own much. All his clothes were already in the duffle bag in his closet, and the few items left around the room were easy to pitch in on top of them. Not having money made it easy to be on the go.

Ready to leave, Jax made one more stop. Jade wasn't being the best sister at the moment, but he was sure she was still in there. He at least owed it to her to let her know he was leaving, and that things were fine. He turned and went into her room, grabbing the notepad off her desk as he entered. Quickly he wrote his message, telling Jade that he would be okay, and she should call if anything was going too badly. He doubted she'd call. She had her new friends after all, and he was just a hunter male. He was only good for following her around and taking orders. That was just one more reason to leave. There wasn't a life left for him with the hunters now that Jade was gone. It was time for him to find his own place in the world.

CHAPTER 2

The drive to New Orleans was quicker than Jax had anticipated. Being a hunter, he only needed a few hours of sleep each night, which meant he could spend more time on the road. The wad of cash in his pocket was enough to get him a place to crash and allow him to be back on his bike before anyone could come looking for him. His mother would either be mad enough to just let him go, or mad enough to come looking for him. He hadn't mentioned in his note to Jade where he was going because he was pretty sure it would be the latter.

And the time alone on the road was good for him. He had been around either his mother or sister for most of his life. They were always telling him what he needed to do and what he needed to improve on. It was hard enough to live with two women, but now it was close to impossible to live with two hunters. Jade had always been there beside him, taking their mother in stride, but now she was acting just like her. Exactly the way Rommy had done to drive them both nuts their whole life, Jade was behaving like a complete butthead of a hunter. There was no way he could continue living like that.

Jax pulled into town by mid-afternoon. It was still light enough that he didn't have to be overly cautious. The local night humans were light sensitive, so he would be free to search around without needing to look over his shoulder. He wasn't there as a hunter, but somehow the night humans always knew who the hunters were. And for the most part, hunters weren't exactly welcome anywhere night humans were. He completely understood, as he had killed more than a couple dozen night humans on his own over the years, not including the group hunts he went on.

Making his way into the French Quarter, he found the hotel he planned to stay at. No more sleeping in a bed that smelled worse than the garbage. No more cramming into a room the size of a closet. He had money, and he was going to use it to stay some place nice for a change. He had no clue who had sent the money, but he would thank them later. For now, he was going to enjoy his vacation from the night human hunter infested world he grew up in.

Jax didn't want to stop without getting the lay of the area. He parked his bike by the beignet shop on the corner and walked a few feet from it. There was a church directly in front of him and two walking pathways going toward it. People milled about the sidewalks, and it even seemed like there were a few people selling things or entertaining the sightseers. Jax stood with the map he had picked up and looked down the street both ways as he orientated himself. The church was the perfect center point to localize by, and from there he picked out more landmarks. New city and new place didn't mean he had to be lost the whole time. A few more glances at the map and around him, and he was pretty sure he had it. Excellent photographic memory was another perk of being a hunter.

Moving to his motorcycle, Jax turned back to the square. He couldn't be completely certain, but it felt like someone was watching him. Jax pretended like he didn't notice as he looked around at all the tourists. The shop he had stopped next to was busy with people coming and going. The nice afternoon weather really brought out the crowd. Jax watched a few and could tell everyone around was human. There wasn't a sign of a night human anywhere. These people were all innocent day humans going about their lives in complete ignorance of the world they actually lived in. So who could be watching him?

New Orleans technically belonged to the Loogaroo night humans. They weren't as sensitive to the sun as other night humans, where any sunlight would instantly burn and kill them, but Loogaroo were still sensitive enough to not like being outside during daylight hours or at lunch time. Jax had chosen to stay in the French Quarter not because they wouldn't be around for the time being, but because the area was neutral ground. Any night human was allowed to walk the tourist-filled area of town as long as they didn't kill there. The exact reason Jax had once traveled to New Orleans in the first place was to find a night human that wasn't following the rules. The Loogaroo clan had hired the hunters themselves.

Jax still felt like someone was watching him. If it wasn't a night human, it could be anyone working for them. While they didn't go outside in daylight, there were many regular humans that associated with night humans and helped them out. Jax didn't need to be on anyone's radar. He wanted to be the one investigating and asking questions, and he didn't have time to get caught up with the night humans and their possible suspicions of him. He wasn't there officially and didn't want to be noticed at all. Anything night human and hunter related would just slow him down. Jax wasn't even sure how long his mother would let him be on his adventure before she came to drag him home.

Hopping back on his bike, Jax took off down the street. The feeling came with him. Whoever was watching him was now following him. The map he had just studied made enough sense for him to crisscross his way back to the hotel he planned to stay at. It was bad enough to be in a new city, but he had to keep an eye out for all the one-ways. Going against traffic wasn't hard on a motorcycle, but it would draw attention to him. His goal now was to blend in and get rid of whoever was following him.

Jax kept driving in circles, which was hopefully keeping whoever was watching him off his tail, and it was giving him a better sense of the area. He had to be sure he wasn't being followed to where he was staying. He was alone in the city, and without someone to take turns on guard duty, he needed to find some way to feel safe, or he'd never get any rest. Without a blinker or warning, Jax swerved into an open driveway for the hotel. He stepped off his bike while slinging his bag around his shoulder and tossing the keys to the valet. His quick exit would hopefully prove too baffling for his pursuer.

Instead of heading inside to check into the hotel, Jax took one last peek outside. He waited in the shadows to see if anyone saw where he'd gone. He almost had to hide his laugh. Night humans were usually the ones slinking in shadows, and now he was doing that exact thing. As he watched the vehicles pass along with the pedestrians, Jax was sure no one had followed him to where he was now. He was safe for the time being.

Stopping at the front desk first, he checked into a room on the top floor with a balcony overlooking the pool. All in all, it was a good escape route if needed; a jump in the pool was a lot less likely to break anything than scaling a wall. Everything was working to his favor. Jax made sure to keep his real driver's license hidden when he checked in. The fake IDs he and his sister got years ago were really handy, because even their mother didn't know about them. He was free to do as he pleased for however long it took to find answers. If his mother made any calls and found out he was in New Orleans, she'd still have to come in person to look for him as long as Jade didn't reveal their secret.

All his time as a hunter had him watching for an escape. He was pretty sure the Loogaroo weren't going to be an issue, but being in a neutral city meant he was probably going to run across a night human or two that did have problems with hunters. Even if they didn't feel his hunter side, one false move and he could be exposed. All hunters from a young age had a tattoo on their forearm, and it was the same for everyone. It was a mark that even the non-night humans could tell and remember. At times Jax wished the tattoo on his forearm was erasable. Then he could walk around just like any other day human, or at least like any other day human that carried a few weapons on them.

Glancing at the sky, Jax saw that the sun still hung plenty high enough. He would have enough time to sleep and do some searching online to find out more about the law firm and bank that the money came from. He doubted it would be as simple as an online search, but he had to look anyway just to be sure. He needed somewhere to start, and it seemed like a good point. It was the start of a new adventure, and Jax was ready to get some answers.

Jax waited until almost lunchtime the next day to venture out of his room. It felt strange to get room service and eat a decent meal before leaving a hotel room, but then again it was also strange to not smell like the bed he rested in. Jax slept an extra hour. There was no reason to rush getting up, and he kind of liked the silence—no mother shouting at something and no sister bossing him around. It was a life he wasn't used to, but could get used to if given enough time.

Jax—dressed in his customary jeans and black, long-sleeved T-shirt—was sure that the looks he was getting were about his choice of long sleeves. It was scorching outside, and the humid air hit him the moment he left the hotel. He could have gone back to change, but long sleeves weren't a fashion statement. It was the only thing he could do to the hide the hunter mark on his arm. At one time he'd been proud to get the matching tattoo with his sister, but now it was a hindrance. He didn't know what he was going to find on his way to the lawyer's office, and he didn't want any trouble before his investigation really began. Hunters never announced official business, and there were sure to be a night human or two around that would see him as a threat.

He had often wished he could trade his life for something different, but some things you couldn't change.

As he approached the ferry, Jax was glad he had spent time looking everything over. It turned out that the return address was an old address for the firm, and they had moved across the river. He would have been walking around quite a while searching for the old office if he hadn't already checked it over. He knew where he was going now. Jax waited for only a moment; he'd arrived with perfect timing, the ferry was still loading and boarding. He climbed aboard and up the stairs to the top deck.

The boat pushed away from shore, and Jax stood at the railing to watch the city skyline. The sun glinted off the tall skyscrapers, and he was once again happy to know he was human instead of a night human like the people he hunted. He couldn't imagine life without being in the sunlight. While several kinds of night humans did have a tolerance for the sun, most didn't, and night human life was exactly what it sounded like: life at night time.

"Out of towner, right?" a female voice asked from beside Jax.

He had felt her approach. She was a normal human, and he didn't look to see who she was. If she'd been a night human, he would have made space between them, but normal day humans weren't an issue.

"I could give you a tour. I've lived here my whole life. I'm Jen."

She offered her hand, and Jax pretended to not hear her as he stared out across the water. He did not need a "tour" or whatever she was really offering. He had a mission that didn't include sightseeing with some girl.

"Want to know how I know?" she continued to talk when Jax didn't respond.

Jax had spent his life having to be friendly for the sake of finding night humans. If he was the first one to talk and offer a hand, he could tell if they were night humans or not. But in reality, it was always an act. He did it because he had to. While night humans could be a problem on his visit, he didn't have to fake friendliness any more. And in reality, cute or not—and she was pretty cute—he didn't want any distractions from his search for answers.

"The shirt," she continued to talk, tossing her auburn curls over her shoulder.

He finally turned to her. It seemed like she wasn't getting the hint that he didn't want to hold a conversation.

"I get cold easily," Jax told her, trying his best to give her his "get lost" face. It had worked on Jade all the time, and on most strangers as well, though this girl obviously wasn't "most" as she leaned toward him instead of away. His look was supposed to be intimidating.

"No. I was more thinking the color. Locals don't walk around dressed like they're vampires unless they work in the Goth shops. You have too much of a tan to work in those shops, so yes, it's the black shirt." The girl smiled at him, happy to finally have his attention, even if his face said get lost.

Jax nodded as his only acknowledgment and moved past her, down the railing farther and closer to the steps. While viewing the city was refreshing, the company wasn't. He was ready to be off the boat and on his way.

"First time in the city?" she asked as she followed. She wasn't getting the hint that he wanted to be alone and that made Jax suspicious. Normal people would have gotten all the hints he was sending her way.

"No," he replied as he headed for the stairs. The shoreline wasn't coming quick enough. Friendly girl was just a bit too coincidental for him.

The girl reached forward and grabbed Jax's sleeve as he moved to walk away. The sleeve slipped a little, and Jax yanked his arm back. He really didn't need anyone seeing the tattoo. He was pretty sure only the edge showed, but he was still looking around the deck to make sure no one noticed. Not looking again at the girl, Jax hurried down the steps away from her. He could feel her eyes on his back, but he wasn't about to sit around and wait for her to expose his whole arm to the people around them. There didn't seem to be any night humans on the boat, but that didn't mean there weren't day humans there that would recognize the mark and tell night humans about him. He didn't have time to deal with the night human drama. He wanted, for once in his life, to just step away from it. He just wanted to find a father, one who had nothing to do with his night human hunting mother. More and more he wanted that life away from it all.

Jax waited at the side of the ferry as it docked. He was alone for now. He could feel the eyes of the girl on him, but he refused to turn around and acknowledge her. She wasn't too far away, but at least she got the hint that he wasn't there to chit-chat.

As soon as he could, Jax hurried off the boat. He had a feeling that the girl was coming closer and would be talking to him again if he didn't. One chance of possibly showing off his hunter status was enough for him to stay clear of her. Whether she did it on purpose or not, he wasn't going to take a second chance with the girl.

Jax took off, sticking to the streets near the river. The Algiers side of New Orleans was quieter than the bustling city side he had just left, and it was actually quiet enough that he could just hear the gurgling of the river as he walked. He was going to need to go a few blocks nearer the river before turning inland toward the address he was heading to. As he found the right street, Jax made his way to the address for Lawrence and Sons. It would be only a block in and on the corner; he had already mapped it out in his head.

Trying not to show surprise, Jax did his best to keep his face neutral as he approached the steps to the law firm. Sitting, like she had been waiting for him to arrive, was the girl from the ferry. Jax walked past her and tried not to acknowledge her as much as he could. He paused long enough to read the name of the firm. It wasn't for Lawrence and Sons, but for Lawrence and Landry. It wasn't the firm he was searching for. His first trip looking for answers and he was hitting a dead end already.

"Not the right place?" she guessed. "Looking for someone else?"

"Henry Lawrence," Jax replied. It wasn't going to be a secret if he was asking around town anyways. Annoying as she was, with any luck on his side the girl might actually be able to point him in the right direction.

"Ahh, Mr. Henry. My Uncle Mike can help you with that. Just follow me." The girl took off in front of him without waiting to see if he was following. The front door was unlocked as she pushed it open and went inside.

"Can I help you?" the lady at the front desk said before glancing up and brightening her smile for the girl that led the way. "Mr. Landry is in a meeting, but I'm sure he'll be happy to see you're early today, Jen."

"Mrs. Summer, can you help this guy? I figured Uncle Mike could sort everything out for him," she told the older secretary.

"Sure thing, sugar. You go on back and make yourself comfortable. I'll let Mr. Landry know you're here."

The girl from the ferry smiled and skipped past Jax, turning to give him a grin on the way. Jax tried not to look, but the nameless girl had become Jen, and someone associated with the people he needed to learn more about. She turned back and walked through a hallway to another part of the building. After finally taking a moment to look at her completely, Jax realized she was much younger than he thought. She couldn't have been more than maybe fifteen, yet somehow fit into everything seamlessly. She was young, but her eyes said otherwise. Jax wondered if his night human radar was off. Maybe he should have shaken her hand after all.

"Sorry about that. We never know when that child will

show up. She's a free spirit, and Mr. Landry can barely keep hold of her." The secretary continued to prattle on like they were old friends. "So what can I help you with?"

"I need to speak to Mr. Lawrence," Jax explained, and the face on the secretary went from a smile to a frown instantly.

"I'm so sorry, son, but Mr. Lawrence has been dead for over six months," she replied.

Jax reached into his pocket. He assumed a letter coming from Henry Lawrence of Lawrence and Sons would actually be from that person. Obviously, he had assumed wrong.

"I received this in the mail the other day. If he's dead, could there be another Henry Lawrence of Lawrence and Sons?" Jax handed the stained envelope over to the gray-haired lady. She only glanced at it before handing it back.

"That's one of his pre-signed ones," she explained, pushing up her glasses. "We had a few accounts that weren't closed when he died, and that's one of them. Mr. Landry can help you with it. Would you like to make an appointment to see him?"

"Would it be possible to just ask him a few questions today? I'm only in town a little while, and it shouldn't take long." Jax turned on his friendly charm. It worked with most people, and he had to try. It wasn't exactly true that he had to leave soon, but if he didn't find answers, he would have to go home and face his mother and sister. The mysterious check would only last so long.

"Let me see." The lady took pity on him as he hoped and picked up the phone.

"Mr. Landry, sorry to disturb you, but I have a young gentleman here that wishes to speak with you today about a letter from Mr. Lawrence. His name is ..." Pausing, the lady peered up at him.

"Jax Kristian," he replied. He had used a fake name to get the hotel room, but this was the one place he knew he had to be honest if he wanted answers.

"Jax Kristian," the lady added. Her face looked surprised as she nodded and *hmm*ed along with whomever was speaking on the other end of the phone. "Sounds good. I'll have him wait in the meeting room."

She hung up the phone and stood up slowly.

"Come this way. He is with a client right now, but he would like to see you today." She led the way behind her desk, and down the hallway, Jen had gone through. Opening a door, she offered Jax a seat at a table. "I don't know how much longer his meeting will be. Would you like something to drink?"

"No, I'm fine," Jax replied, sitting down at the table.

The lady nodded and walked back the way they came. There was no more of an explanation or an answer, but it was something. Hopefully, Mr. Landry would be able to answer more questions for him.

Jax was alone and tempted to look around the room or maybe the office, but he remembered that technically he wasn't by himself. Jen was somewhere in the same general area, and he didn't want to get caught snooping. It had to be the hunter in him that was curious. They were sending him letters with money from someone who had been dead six months. That was strange, but the girl was even more of a puzzle. It was like she knew he was going to the same place as her.

"You know, if you wanted to get my name, all you had to do was ask," Jen said as she entered the room and sat down across from him.

Jax rolled his eyes. He couldn't help it. At that exact moment, the girl sounded exactly like Jade. Heck, she looked a little like his sister with the same blue eyes that he shared with Jade, but brunette to Jade's actual natural blonde that had been dyed every color possible over the years. He wasn't sure what color his sister's hair would be by the time he got home. It seemed to change almost weekly lately.

"Jax. Now that's an odd name. I've never met a Jax

before," Jen continued. And that was completely different, too. Jade wasn't outgoing. But there was something about her that still reminded him of his sister.

Jax simply stared at her. He wanted to know more about the law firm, but he didn't want to ask too much since he wasn't sure who she was or how she was related to everything. Yes, he was a little paranoid, but anyone who met his mother understood why. Legendary Rommy had a sixth sense about everything, and was a master at playing games to get what she wanted. She wasn't the best hunter simply because of her combat skills. It was her mind that made her who she was, and Jax couldn't help but view the world as if everyone was the same way.

"So I heard you're here to see my uncle." Jen continued to offer up information. That was helpful, but still didn't make him trust her, no matter how helpful she was, or how much she reminded him of Jade.

"I've been told that much," Jax replied. Maybe if he kept her talking, then she would offer more without him having to ask. He could play the game even if he wasn't as good as his mother.

"Good luck getting him to stop talking. Uncle Mike likes to talk. This is probably still his one o'clock meeting two hours later. That's typical of him. So what are you here for? Some sort of secret meeting, or is it the typical boring stuff?"

Jax could see there was a talking gene in the family, and it didn't seem to be only her uncle.

"Boring stuff," Jax replied. "But what sort of secret meetings does he do?"

Jen jumped up just as someone passed the open doorway. She grinned at Jax before leaving the way she came. She sure was an odd person. Jax still wasn't certain what to make of her. One moment she was helping him, and the next she was disappearing. Jax was used to weird people in the night human world, but he wasn't used to normal humans being just as odd.

Jax was pretty sure he had waited over an hour before anyone came back into the room. Jen never showed up again, but that was fine. He was back to suspecting she had some sort of ulterior motive. In reality, she probably didn't, but he couldn't be too safe.

While he waited, he had walked around the room more than once. He was pretty sure that there was only an office on the one side of the room, as slightly muffled sounds came from one direction. He had listened to the front door down the hall and never once heard the bell that announced someone had entered. It was a small office with not many clients. None of it explained the check. Jax had calculated how much money there would have to be to send a check that size for his whole life, and he was pretty sure that someone with money like that wouldn't go to a small dive of a law firm like this. Well, not unless they had to. That was part of the story Jax was guessing was more than a little true. You either used a small, out-of-the-way place like this because you were doing shady business, or because you lived in that shade. As much as he wanted to get away from the night humans, the whole office set up, and the money made him have a strong feeling he wasn't done with them yet.

"Sorry for the wait, but if you could please follow me, dear," the older secretary said as she appeared in the doorway.

Jax stood from where he had just sat back down. He was lucky he had. He hadn't heard the lady approach. He'd been too busy listening in and trying to make out words on the other side of the wall. It would have been too embarrassing to have gotten caught standing there with his ear to the wall. At least seated he looked natural.

The secretary led Jax down the hallway away from where

he had entered. As they stopped at an open door, he casually glanced around. He saw that the corridor turned and led to a back doorway, but there was nothing else as he suspected. It really was a small place.

"Mr. Landry, here is Jax Kristian," she told him, motioning for Jax to come in and sit down.

"Jax," Mr. Landry said as he stood and shook Jax's hand.

Human. That much was obvious, even if he hadn't just confirmed it with a handshake. Jax had been only a small child when he first realized that he could tell who was a night human from a handshake, but no one could tell him why. All the other hunters were just as baffled by it as his mother was. That was why he decided to keep these new "possible future outcome" visions from her. She had lots of questions about the harpy hunt, but she believed all his vague answers, especially with Jade's support. He didn't want to go another round with the hunters all gossiping about him, or worse would be them testing it out. He really didn't want to die over and over again by their hand just to show them how it worked. He had a feeling his life would never be the same once they knew.

"I came here looking for a Mr. Lawrence, but was informed that he has passed," Jax cut right to the chase. If this guy really did like to talk, it could be dark by the time he left, and that wasn't a good thing. He only had a couple weapons on him. He would have loved to pick the older man's brain a bit if it were earlier in the evening, but not now.

"Yes. Dear old Henry died over six months ago. He'd been sick for weeks, but just couldn't make it any longer. We were lucky he lasted long enough to transfer everything over to me. I've been working with him for over a decade, but he still called most of the shots," Landry continued on. Jax nodded his head as much as he could, but talkative people drove him nuts when he was focused on something, and right now he was focused.

"Would you be able to help me with this then?" Jax took the envelope out of his pocket and spoke quickly when Landry paused to take a breath.

Landry took the envelope and stared at it. He nodded his head, but his face said he already knew what it meant. The one time Jax hoped he would be talkative, the man went silent.

"Let me go check and see which file this belongs to," Landry stated as he stood up and walked out of the room.

Why in the world would a lawyer need to leave his own office to check a file? Warnings were going off for Jax, and he didn't need to be a hunter to know things weren't adding up. The office alone was making his hunter side go wary, but this man was even worse. Rising, Jax slowly approached the door. Years of training made his steps silent—you couldn't be running around chasing night humans who had super hearing if they could pick up your movements. Jax paused just inside the doorway. He didn't need to go further; the man speaking down the hall was clear as day.

"He's asking about Henry and has this," Landry said to someone.

"Then you'll talk to him just like everyone else, and we'll wait. I already informed them that he was here. You've been great at stalling already. They should be here in twenty minutes at the most," the secretary told him. Her voice was no longer cheerful, and actually, the way she spoke made Jax wonder which one of them was really in charge.

"But what if he—" Landry began, but stopped suddenly.

"Mr. Cunningham is out of town, but I'm sure he will be back soon. He will want to deal with this himself. No failing. Just talk to the kid until they arrive," she told him, and it seemed that it wasn't so much a suggestion as an order.

Jax hurried back to his chair and sat down as Landry came back down the hallway. Jax pretended like he hadn't heard.

"Sorry about that. I've got the file right here," Landry

held up a yellow filing folder. He opened it to the first page. Jax couldn't see what was written on it, but he was willing to give the lawyer a few more minutes before bolting. He wasn't about to stick around and see who was coming once the sun had set enough for them to go outside. "So, just to be sure we have this all in order, you are Jaxton Kristian, right?"

"Yes," Jax replied.

"And your birthday is August 14th?" he asked, reading from the file.

So he had some information. Jax was now more intrigued. He needed to leave, but wanted to know more.

"That would be me," Jax replied, and then waited. He wasn't going to spend time talking. He wanted the lawyer to do that.

"Good. Then I have the right case file," Landry replied, but then fell silent.

"And could you tell me a little more?" Jax actually had to ask.

"No, actually. The rest of the file is sealed. I don't have permission to read or unseal it. If you were eighteen, I could hand it over to you, but since you're a minor, either your parents or the person who left this file will need to release it to you."

Shoot. That isn't about to happen. Jax hadn't left his mother a note to tell her where he was going or if he was returning. Not that it mattered much. He brought his phone with him, and neither his mother nor sister had called once since he left. He knew how important he was to the hunter family, and was pretty sure there would be a whole group already hauling him home if he had been a girl. His male genes made him disposable, and there was no way his mother would travel to New Orleans to let him have a file a few months early. Heck, from the look of it, more than likely she was hoping he'd never see it in the first place.

"So who gave you the file? Could that person be

contacted?" Jax was curious as to what else was in the folder.

"He's out of town at the moment, but I think we could draft a letter to fax him and maybe we could get this all straightened out," Landry explained, turning to his computer and starting to type.

Jax nodded. This was his stellar plan to stall him into waiting until dark? That wasn't about to happen. It seemed like Landry was done talking and giving out information. Jax was going to have to dig elsewhere or perhaps get involved with the local night humans. He was still planning to avoid the night humans at all costs.

"Do you have a restroom I can use?" Jax asked. That was innocent enough. They'd had him waiting forever, so he was bound to need one eventually.

Landry glanced up from his computer screen.

"Yes, it's across the hallway from the conference room. Just take a right into the hall and then a left into the restroom." Landry returned his gaze to the computer screen.

That was all Jax needed to know, and he was gone. He turned to the restroom and doubled back to make it out the back door. Slightly worried that an alarm would go off, he took his time opening it, but nothing happened. Now he needed to get back to the ferry. He wasn't staying around to meet the welcoming party. He would be happy to go back to his hotel and wait out the night. No one would find a Jax Kristian in any hotel in the area. He'd picked up his second ID with Jade years ago so they could get into clubs and bars while they were both underage. He would have to thank her later, but for the remainder of the night, he was going to look more into the lawyer that originally did his case. His instincts were telling him that there was something he was missing here, and Lawrence was the hand that signed all the checks.

CHAPTER 3

The night had been as uneventful as he expected it to be since he had hidden himself well. No night humans came knocking, and he spent most of the time looking up information on Henry Lawrence. The man had been older, but not old. He was in his late fifties, and everything said he had died of a massive heart attack. Nothing mentioned him being sick for a long time, and Landry's story didn't make sense. How could a man that had died of a sudden heart attack have time to sort and move all his cases over to another lawyer? Was it because the case had money involved that Landry took it and was making up a story about getting it, or did Lawrence not die of a heart attack? Something wasn't right, and Jax had a plan.

All the papers indicated that Henry had been interred at a local mausoleum. If Jax's suspicions were correct, then Henry might not actually be in his final resting spot. Jax had been on way too many night human hunts over the years, and when things didn't add up, it had something to do with the undead suckers.

Jax had checked, and double checked the time when the place would close before he took off with more than just a couple weapons this time. With two strapped to his legs, one on his wrist, and two more in his pant pockets, he felt safe enough. He hadn't been expecting trouble with night humans the day before, but he was beginning to see there was a new theme in his life. He could never really get away from them, and he was pretty sure it wasn't the fault of the tattoo on his forearm.

Driving not too far away was the plan since he didn't want to be left without an escape. Yesterday he had to leave on foot, and that wouldn't have worked well if he had been caught with a night human. He was a fast runner, but not as fast as the leeches. A car would have been preferable as it could get you away and keep you covered, but since he only had his motorcycle, it would have to do for the time being. Jax made it over to the mausoleum with plenty of time to wait and to get the perfect parking spot. He wasn't excited to sit in the humid heat, but it was his only option. He needed to enter just before closing.

The large, gray, stone building took up the entire block. He could see the entrance from where he was parked, yet he still leaned against his bike and waited. He'd grown up as a hunter, and one thing all hunters were good at was waiting. Timing could be everything. The wait was hot, but necessary. Jax was more than willing to sit and work through his plan mentally.

Taking a deep breath, it was time to go check out his hunch. While he didn't want to be right, he had a feeling that there was going to be more to investigate either way it turned out. At least he didn't have to walk through the above-ground tombs. Too many evenings fighting things that went bump in the night made him not appreciate above-ground tombs at all. He knew of a few clans that liked to make them their daytime resting place, and he didn't want to interrupt a bloodsucker in its den.

Casually strolling toward the entrance, Jax made it seem like he was sure he belonged there. Taking the first right into the marbled hallway, Jax waited for someone to come around and tell him to leave. The only person that passed was a janitor who didn't give him a second look. After what seemed like well past closing time, he was sure he heard someone finally coming near. He knew Henry's body wasn't in the wing he was standing in, but he needed to pretend he was lost to get the worker to lead him to the right place. They would drop their guard enough to allow him to stay past closing. Jax turned and pretended to search the names on the wall of tombs in front of him.

Warnings went off in Jax's mind ... hunter warnings. Jax turned in time to block the man that pounced at him like a cat on a mouse. Jax didn't need to see the fangs extended to know it was a night human. Jax was happy his night human sensing skills were getting better, or he would have been dead. He wasn't expecting to run into a night human inside the building and around all the dead bodies. Night humans always fed on live bodies, so a mausoleum wasn't really their scene.

Blocking a punch headed his way that contained awfully large claws, Jax ducked down to grab the stake in his shoe. He didn't have time to analyze what type of night human was attacking him as he was pretty sure it planned to make him its supper. Jax dropped the weight of the second arm that came close to his head and ducked down, getting the proper position to stand and thrust the wood into the night human. Different ways worked best with different types of night humans, but one thing was always the same—a stake to the heart would kill just about anything. Well, that and lopping off a head. His mother preferred to take heads, but Jax wasn't one to wander around with a sword strapped to his back. They were harder to hide than his mother made it seem, and blending in was one of Jax's best strengths.

Blending in and appearing just a normal human probably was the only thing that saved Jax's life as he pushed the stake deep into the monster attacking him. The creature let out a surprised gurgle before it instantly turned to ash. Jax stared at the pile of ash-covered clothing. At least there was one answer. He knew what kind of night human it was now. And that just led to more questions. It was a vampyre, and from what he'd learned the last time he was in Louisiana, he was pretty sure this was the first sighting of a vampyre by a hunter in over a couple decades. He had been taught that they were pretty much extinct, but the pile of dust at his feet would prove otherwise.

Jax looked up as the janitor he saw cleaning before pushed a cart with trash toward Jax. *How much had he seen?* Jax quickly tried to think up an excuse for the ashes at his feet.

"I'll get that mess for you. You made my job much easier," the older man said as he neared. He was ready to sweep up the ashes and clothing. It turned out that Jax didn't need an excuse after all.

"Easier?" Jax was kind of afraid to ask. The man didn't look like he was a hunter in his free time. Hunters typically didn't live to his age.

"The newbies always like to tear apart visitors. They get excited with their first taste of blood, so it happens more often than anyone that runs this place likes to admit," he explained as if it was completely normal for a night human to attack in the mausoleum. "They say dead bodies are good for business."

The old janitor wiped his forehead with a handkerchief from his shirt pocket before pulling out a broom to sweep the mess up with.

"Yes, I like this much better. Would you like to stop by more often around dusk and take care of this sort of mess for me?" He then laughed as he picked up the clothing and tossed it into his trash can, dropping more dust on the ground in the process.

"This happens that often?" Jax cautiously asked. They really had no reports of vampyre activity in New Orleans, and nothing of them ripping up innocents in town. This was the sort of thing that got reported to the clans and the hunters. Bloodthirsty night humans were kind of their specialty to destroy.

The old janitor rubbed his short gray hair. "Hmm. More lately. I'd say about once or twice a week." He continued to sweep up the mess on the marble floor.

"And no one reports this?" If the old man knew about night humans, then he should have known about telling someone that rogue night humans were there killing people.

"The owners of the mausoleum are paid well for letting this happen here. If I report, I'll be out of a job. At least this way I can continue to work." He gave a small shrug before bending down with the dust pan.

"And you don't worry that they'll attack you one of these times?" It was Jax's curiosity that made him ask.

The man smiled, showing off perfectly straight teeth. "They don't touch a man of God." He reached inside his shirt and pulled out a carved wooden cross. "The Loogaroo don't hunt in the city. It's only the vampyre, and their laws mean that I'm safe."

Jax nodded. The janitor confirmed that it really was a vampyre that Jax had just killed. He was going to have to go back to the hotel and check to be sure on everything regarding the vamprye. He remembered a bit about them, but since none had been seen in decades, he hadn't studied much on them lately.

The janitor finished sweeping up the last of the vampyre and stood up to stare at Jax.

"From your moves, I expect that you're what they call a hunter," the man said. He looked Jax up and down, like he was a new thing to study. "I've never seen one myself, and they tend to police themselves around here, but I've heard of you guys. Born as strong as night humans, but not being one of them. We could use a few of you around here."

"I thought you said they keep track of their own," Jax asked. Wasn't that what the man just said?

"Oh, they do punish offenders, but let's just say one night human judging another night human doesn't benefit anyone but night humans. They don't always seem to have a good sense of right and wrong, such as they don't always punish their kind for killing a normal human. We're just food, after all. I think we'd do better with normal humans like you and your kind around, but they refuse to call in the hunters. They've refused for years."

"They?"

The old man just scratched his chin. "I think I've said enough already." He turned back to his rolling trash can and broom, and moved to walk away.

"I'm actually not here hunting," Jax said to his back. "I'm looking for a lawyer named Henry Lawrence. He was entombed here about six months ago."

The janitor stopped. "And you want to know if he's really here," he verbalized what Jax was thinking, but not asking.

Jax had a suspicion before coming to the mausoleum, but he hadn't needed to know if the lawyer was really dead or not. He just needed to know where to find him if he was alive. But being a vampyre and being alive were two different things. The one fact that Jax was sure about with the vampyre was that they couldn't have children like other night humans. The only way to become one was to turn someone into one, which was why the hunters assumed they were extinct. New vampyre would feed and leave a trail to follow. They hadn't seen that since before Jax was alive. If Henry was one now, there would be a trail.

"I can help you with that, but you don't need to go breaking into a tomb to find out the truth. I knew Henry, and I know he's no longer here." The janitor turned back around. "I watched him walk out that doorway three days after they put his body in its final resting place. He had been my friend for over thirty-five years. He was a good man, a God-fearing man. But Henry Lawrence is now undead and no longer able to be saved."

Jax nodded as he walked past the older janitor who was frozen in his spot and in his memories. It saved time to not have to go breaking into a tomb, and Jax was happy to not be walking around the above-ground cemeteries that were all over the city. However, he didn't like what it meant. No matter how much he wanted to get away from the night human world, Jax was getting pulled right back to it. Now he was going to have to go night human hunting to get his answers. For that, he'd need more weapons.

Jax quickly made it back to the hotel to stock up on his weapons before heading out to follow the directions of the janitor. Henry Lawrence lived outside of town in an old mansion that his family had owned for over a century. Jax knew he was pushing it close, and he would have less than an hour at most to get away from it to be safe. He drove way over the speed limit and made his way to the address. Turning off the road onto the gravel pathway, he could see that the house wasn't too far away.

The picturesque trees swaying in the breeze matched the two-story yellow house, and made it feel a bit like stepping back in time. It seemed not much had changed in the hundred years that the Lawrence family had owned the place. Jax stopped his bike and sat for a moment, just looking around. It was quiet outside of the city, but it was an eerie quiet. He expected to hear something, but there was complete silence.

Walking carefully toward the house, Jax stopped on the rocking-chair-lined porch. It wasn't the safest to be walking up to a house when he had no idea what inhabited it, but he was certain that Henry Lawrence would have answers.

Knocking at the door first, Jax waited. The screen door was closed, but the inside of the house was visible. There was no one inside. He waited a little longer. Why would someone leave the house completely open without being around? Jax turned back to walk around the grounds. Circling the house, Jax made it to the backdoor. He could see in from this direction too and discovered that nothing was moving inside the house. The place was empty.

Jax debated what to do. He could go inside and explore, possibly running across the old owner, or he could wait and see if anyone came back. Someone could still live there.

From the obituary, Jax knew that Henry had a wife and children. Maybe someone was home or out in the yard somewhere. Jax opted to walk back around to the front of the house again, hoping either someone would come to the door or be standing outside.

Raising a fist to knock one more time, Jax froze in place as he felt someone move inside the house. That wasn't a good sign. Jax didn't feel normal humans, only night humans. There was someone in there, but they weren't answering. Possibly they were the reason why there was no one around. Jax could feel the night human presence inside as it headed upstairs.

"Hi there," a middle-aged man said from behind Jax.

Jax whipped around, already sensitive from what he knew was inside the house. He kept his stance as relaxed as he could, even though he felt the threat of what he was going to face. The man staring at him wasn't Henry Lawrence, and he wasn't a night human. For all Jax knew the man didn't even realize what was inside the house, or possibly he had talked to Henry and didn't understand he was no longer human.

"I was looking for the house of the Lawrence family," Jax said as truthfully as he could. Not only was he looking for family to ask questions to, but also for the older man in the process.

"I'm sorry, son, but they left on a trip a couple days ago. They don't plan to be back until next week," he explained. "I'm Charlie. I take care of the grounds and watch over the house while the Lawrences are gone."

"I'm a classmate of Will's from school," Jax fibbed. Sometimes his age came in handy. "He said he was going to leave a book for me, and that I could stop by anytime to pick it up."

Charlie laughed. "I bet he would love it if you took all his books. That child has never liked school. He'd much rather be out playing ball. You can go see if he left it out. They left in a rush, so I don't know if he would have remembered something like that."

"You saw them leave?" Jax asked, his curiosity piqued. Empty house and sudden family vacation didn't add up to anything good in Jax's book.

"No. They left at night time while no one was here, but I saw and picked up the mess they left, inside and out. Mrs. Lawrence will be happy I found her necklace outside in the driveway. That's how I know they were rushed. She would never leave without it. Mr. Lawrence gave it to her when they were teens."

Jax nodded as Charlie moved up the stairs and opened the door to the house. Jax followed behind him. He could feel the presence of a night human in the house, but there still wasn't a single sound.

"Kind of eerie out here alone," Jax commented as Charlie walked to the staircase.

"Only for a few days. Then they will be back, and those boys don't know the meaning of quiet," Charlie joked. He had no clue there was someone in the house. The only question was how long they had been there and if it was the person Jax was looking for. Jax was a little wary of leaving Charlie alone. "Will's room is the first door at the top of the stairs. Good luck finding the book." Charlie grinned and left Jax to go upstairs on his own. Jax kind of wondered if he should make an excuse to not go upstairs, but so far the night human was staying in one place.

Jax climbed the stairs and tapped on the stake hidden beneath his sleeve as he did so. It looked like it wasn't a one night human sort of day after all.

Opening the door to the first room slowly, Jax now understood why Charlie wished him luck. The room was a disaster. Jax wasn't sure where to step to walk into the room. He doubted a night human would be hidden amongst all the stuff littering the floor and walls. Jax just smiled. Jade would have been that messy growing up if they actually owned stuff. With all the moving they did, they never had a chance to hold on to anything, never mind leave stuff around like that. Jax shook his head. He didn't need thoughts of missing his sister to break his concentration.

Slowly, Jax made it across the room. He didn't feel the night human in the room, but it was still upstairs. Walking over to the desk in the corner and the stuff thrown around, he grabbed a book. Not that the kid would notice in the mess. His excuse for visiting was covered.

Jax made his way back across the room as he didn't want to stay and search the teen's room. What he really needed was to search the father's room, but the house was too squeaky for him to find an easy way to get down the hallway without Charlie coming up. Since Jax was sure the night human was hiding out upstairs, he didn't want to bring a day human up if he didn't have to. He would just get in the way if the sucker decided to attack.

At the bottom of the stairs, Charlie was already standing and waiting.

"Perfect timing," Charlie said to Jax as he climbed down. "I need to head back to my place, and I was hoping I wouldn't have to wait all night for you to find the book you needed."

Smiling, he tapped the book in his hand. "It was waiting just where Will said he would leave it."

Jax walked toward the doorway, and Charlie followed. Once out the door, Charlie turned and locked the place, the night human still inside.

"Done for the day?" Jax asked casually.

"Yes, and ready to go home and get some dinner," Charlie replied as he walked down the stairs and to Jax's bike with him.

Jax looked around. There was a gravel driveway leading to the place, but his was the only vehicle there. Off to the side was some sort of barn or shed, but that was closed, too. He was a bit curious how Charlie was getting home. It was getting dark out, and with one bloodsucker in the house, Jax was worried that the man was going to be night human food before the evening was done.

"I live just beyond those trees there," Charlie explained as Jax looked around. "My family has been taking care of this place almost as long as it has been here."

Jax threw his leg over his bike.

"Hopefully Will will be home soon, and I can return the book to him," Jax commented as he started the engine.

Charlie backed up and waved to him. "I'd say don't worry about it. I've never seen Will open a book, so he probably won't miss it." He laughed again as he stepped farther away.

Jax could see a worn path from the house into the surrounding woods.

"Thanks again," Jax said as he glanced at the house. It might have been wishful thinking, but he could almost swear he saw someone in one of the upstairs windows. Charlie waved to Jax as he started down the driveway back to the main road.

There were still too many questions that he couldn't answer. Jax had a feeling he was heading to the right spots, but he also needed to find the right people. He kind of wished Charlie hadn't been there, and he could have explored the house more. He couldn't put the man in any danger, but it wouldn't exactly be danger for Jax. He had already taken care of one vampyre today, what was one more? Charlie was probably home now, and the house was locked up. But that didn't mean Jax couldn't explore.

Jax had only driven for about ten minutes before turning around. It was slowly getting darker. Night humans would be free to roam soon, and it was probably a stupid idea to go back to a place where he knew there was one, but it was his only lead so far. He'd just have to be cautious and remember everything he could about the vampyre.

After walking around the house at least three more times, Jax was sure that the night human was gone. But where would it go? It was barely dark so it couldn't move freely yet, and there were the questions about who it was. Was it Henry Lawrence or someone associated with him or his law firm? Why did the night human leave? Did he know Jax was a hunter? Was he afraid? More questions without answers. Jax wanted to wear a sign saying he wasn't hunting so that maybe he would have more luck.

Jax got the sense that there was still a night human lurking around. He had never tried to track one with just his ever-growing sense of night humans, but it was worth a try. Closing his eyes, he concentrated on the feeling. It was easier than he thought it would be. He could feel it like a compass. The night human was directly behind the house, toward the trees. Jax opened his eyes, and in the fading light, he saw a small trail leading away from the house. If he had not been sensing the night human, he wouldn't have seen it.

Now was the real question: was it safe to hunt a night human on his own? He had taken care of night humans when they'd been on missions, but everything was planned. He had never gone off on a mission alone, and he was certainly not allowed to confront a night human on his own while hunting for the hunters. Only full-fledged hunters could take solo missions. Every night human he had ever killed had been because he had to—ordered to or it was attacking him. Now it was a choice. No one was threatening his life, and he was free to just walk away. It truly was a choice this time.

Jax hesitated only a moment before heading off toward the trees. Choice or not, he wanted answers. Because of that, his decision was made for him. He didn't need to kill the night human, and hopefully, it would understand that much. That night human out there possibly had an answer or two.

Years of training came in handy as Jax walked through

the woods. It was easy to walk and not make any noise, which was extremely helpful during tracking. He wanted to get close enough to see who the night human was. He had a hunch that it was Henry, but he wasn't certain. Jax didn't want to mess around with any other night human. Continuing farther away from the house and his getaway bike, he had to hope the path didn't lead to any swamps or alligators. Night humans were easy to fight, but Jax wasn't a fan of fighting nature or reptiles.

Just when he thought he would be close enough to see the night human, the trail stopped. He felt it before he could turn around, and in an instant, the night human was gone again. Jax stood alone in the darkening night in the middle of the woods, behind a house no one knew he had gone to visit. Not the best plan, but he was close enough to where he should have met the mysterious night human. Turning around, he viewed the area with the last of the setting sun's rays. It was just an open area of grass in the middle of the woods. There wasn't much there at all. The space wasn't that large. If it was an ambush spot, it would be perfect, except that the night human had run away. Jax was confused as he looked around until his eyes adjusted to the darkness. In front of him were three mounds of earth, like something had been recently buried there.

Jax stood over the first lump in the ground. It was long and wide enough to be something he really didn't want to see. There was a reason he was relieved to not walk in the tombs of the cemetery before when he went looking for Henry Lawrence. He wasn't a fan of the freshly killed, and even less of a fan of the freshly risen. The earthen mound was the perfect size to fit a human body underneath. Jax checked the trees and picked the best one. He didn't want to stick around, but he couldn't let a new night human attack some unknowing human. Jax didn't want to be a hunter, but he felt like he had to protect everyone nonetheless.

With only a small jump, Jax caught a branch and pulled

himself up. If this was a tomb of a vamprye that was going to rise, he wanted to be around to stop it from hurting anyone. Jax climbed high enough that his scent should be hidden in the smell of the leaves, but still close enough to the ground to be able to get closer to the night human once it had risen. Jax settled in his spot to sit and wait. He couldn't remember if they rose right after sunset, or another specific time in the night.

Darkness settled on the woods, and Jax wasn't surprised in the least at the lack of light. He had been all over the US to hunt bad night humans. He had moved from city to city his whole life, and some of the towns had only a few street lamps. It was dark where there weren't a lot of people. And besides, he was used to the dark. Night humans were most active in the dark, and therefore so were the hunters. He had lived his whole life knowing about bloodsuckers. All the bad fairy tales weren't just stories to him; they were real.

Jax tapped the side of the tree like he was playing the strings of his guitar. Waiting was part of the job he was used to and the part that he actually liked. It was quiet in the woods with only the chirp of crickets and croaks of frogs. Jax preferred the company of nature to people. He spent so much time pretending to be a people person that being alone was refreshing. The wait could be any amount of time, but it seemed like it was going to be short this time around.

Sensing the night human that approached before he could see it, Jax closed his eyes and used his other senses. It would be great to have the night human sense of seeing in the dark, but because he didn't, Jax had strengthened his other senses. His hearing and sense of feeling the night human were strong with his eyes closed. He could even make out the blur as the night human moved through the forest.

The night human was moving toward him fast, but still trying to be cautious to not be heard. Maybe he thought Jax was still following him. Jax could have laughed at that. All the other animals in the forest sensed the abnormal creature also, and had either grown silent or fled. Quiet as could be wasn't quiet enough to fool nature.

The night human came closer and was soon standing in the small clearing. Jax opened his eyes and stared down at the man standing beside one of the mounds of dirt. There was enough light for Jax to make out the night human's face. He didn't hesitate, but dropped down in front of him.

"Glad to see you aren't dead after all, Mr. Lawrence," Jax said as he looked directly at the man. Jax could tell he seemed to be contemplating whether he should flee or not. "You're a hard man to find."

CHAPTER 4

Jax waited while the not-so-dead lawyer internally debated what to do. The man remained frozen as his eyes darted around like he was trying his best to come up with a response. Jax could see that he wanted to run, but something was keeping him there. His feet remained frozen to the ground, and panic was easy to read on his face. If it weren't for the three mounds of dirt, Jax was pretty sure the man would be long gone already. It was possible that Henry might even still flee. Jax needed to disarm him and make him understand that he wasn't there to hunt him.

"So I'm guessing these will rise tonight?" Jax began the conversation, sure that it wasn't going to happen unless he said something.

Henry Lawrence appeared genuinely shocked that Jax had guessed that much. Jax really needed to tread carefully with the night human. He held up his hands to show he didn't have a weapon.

"I've never seen a night human being reborn, but I've read about it and taken tests on it," Jax explained. "It's not the kind of thing they take us on field work to do."

Now the lawyer was very confused. He obviously sensed Jax was dangerous, but he didn't know what he was talking about. Jax was relieved, but he knew he had to tell the man the truth.

"My mother is Rommy Kristian. I took this trip to Louisiana to get some answers from you, only to find out you were already dead. No one has ever told me a single thing about my father, but then my hopes were dashed as soon as I went to your office. You don't look too dead to me," Jax added.

"I'd have died if it wasn't for being turned into this," he explained.

"This being a …" Jax trailed off, hoping Mr. Lawrence would fill in the blanks with the answer he already suspected. He knew the man was a night human, but he needed to confirm what kind.

"A vampyre. I was dying from cancer, and luckily enough my master deemed me worth saving," Henry explained. He was still watching Jax like a hawk, and keeping his body between the hunter and the piles of dirt. His resolve seemed more determined now that Henry knew who Jax was.

"And you're waiting for someone to rise. Can I guess?" Jax didn't need to guess.

There were three mounds of dirt and three people who mysteriously took off in the middle of the night on an unannounced trip. In reality, it wasn't a very bright plan to be sitting around a spot where potentially three new hungry night human would be arising soon, but Jax wasn't one to back down when close to an answer.

Henry Lawrence moved a step closer to Jax with a growl coming from the back of his throat. He felt threatened. Jax didn't move, but stared at the vampyre. The lawyer might have been a night human, but he had been older when he became one. He would be slower than what the hunters normally chased, and possibly even weaker. Jax had trained to fight the top of the night human ladder, not the bottom. Henry wasn't much of a threat. Jax wasn't afraid of the man standing before him, but he also needed answers from him. That left two choices: take him down and try to force an answer out, or play nice.

"I'm not here on official hunter business, and I really don't care that you changed your whole family into night humans. That's between your maker and you. What I came here for was to get some answers. I'm going to reach into my pocket to get an envelope. That's all."

Jax slowly and calmly reached into his pants pocket. New night humans, in general, were jumpy the first few years. They thought everyone, especially hunters, were there to kill them.

After unfolding the paper, Jax held it out for the older man to take. Henry's eyes looked him up and down as he contemplated whether to come closer and take it from him or not. Jax didn't move and patiently waited. He had to be calm, no matter how jumpy the man in front of him was. In a flash, Henry stepped forward, took the paper, and stepped back again. If his senses weren't heightened, Jax would have never noticed the man moving.

Henry stood in his place in front of the tombs and looked at the dirty envelope. He read it more than once without saying a word. Jax took that as an indication to talk more.

"My name is Jax Kristian, and you sent this to me. I assume, by the notation on the check, this isn't the first one sent to me, but it's the first one I've ever seen. My mother had been throwing them away. I want to know why you're sending me money, and what it means."

Henry now squinted at Jax. Reaching into his pocket, he took out glasses before looking back down at the paper in his hand, like his glasses would help him put the puzzle together.

"You're Jaxton?" the man said as he finally turned back up. "You're really Jaxton Cunningham, Rommy's son?"

Jax stared at the man. His last name was certainly not Cunningham, but the lawyer seemed positive that it was.

"Jax Kristian," Jax corrected. He was pretty sure the envelope said that anyway.

"Right, sorry. Jax Kristian, son of Rommy Kristian." Henry put his glasses away. His stance relaxed as he viewed Jax.

"So why do you send me money, or rather your old partner sends me money now?"

"You went to see Michael?"

"Yes, my first stop was there ... until I realized that he was knee-deep in night humans. He has a night human secretary," Jax stated his suspicion as truth. "I really didn't want to have to deal with night humans at all. This was supposed to be a 'find out where the money comes from' trip and maybe finally get some info on my father, but it changed the moment I went into that office."

"As a hunter, do you think your life will ever be night human free?" Henry asked rhetorically.

Jax shrugged. He had been thinking more and more about life without being a hunter. He didn't want to give up his family, as dysfunctional as it was, and it would be hard to pretend he knew nothing about the night human world, but he just couldn't see where he fit in any of it any more. He loved his sister and didn't want anything to happen to her, but he didn't want to be bossed around by her for the rest of his life, either. It had only been days since his life as a night human hunter, but he was finding that he didn't miss it at all.

"I just want to know who's sending me the money and why," Jax explained, not answering the question.

"I'm not sure you really want to know. If you went to Michael, then he had the answer for you," Henry explained.

"He had a folder with information on me, but he never told me who the money came from, why I'm getting it, or what it means," Jax clarified. Hence the reason he went looking for Henry Lawrence, but he didn't add that. "My mother told me nothing growing up. She's never mentioned my father or where his family is from. I have no idea why or where the money comes from, but I assume it is him. This is the first time in my life that I have any sort of information on that half of my family."

Henry moved over to sit against a tree. Jax was happy to see that the older man didn't view him as a threat any longer. Jax was serious that he didn't care in the least that the man had turned his family. Yes, Jax wanted to protect day humans, but the man's family was something different. If he turned them, it was because he wanted to keep them as his family. Jax wasn't there to judge him on that. Night humans lived by the rules of their clan. If their clan did something really bad, the hunters would be called in, but for the most part night humans were allowed to live as they liked.

Jax leaned back against the tree he was standing by, trying to mimic the relaxed stance of the older man.

"I'm sure that the folder is back in the safe by now. If he didn't tell you, then it was because he was told he couldn't. Your father put an order on the file that it couldn't be disclosed without his permission until you turned eighteen. Then you wouldn't need permission," Henry stated exactly what the other lawyer had told him.

Jax kept his mouth shut instead of swearing. Was it really his fault he wouldn't be eighteen for a couple more months? That was a ridiculous rule. He was in town now, and he couldn't guarantee he would be around in two months. Why was that number important? Sure it made him an adult, but as far as Jax could see, he'd been an adult for years. His mother hadn't taken care of him or Jade since Jade had turned into a teenager.

"And I suppose you won't tell me either? Lawyer-client confidentially stays after death?" Jax already knew the answer by the expression on the guy's face. He wasn't going to give him the information from that file, either.

Henry shook his head. "I'm not dead."

Jax shrugged. Close enough. True, night humans weren't actually dead, but since they had to survive on human blood, it made them close enough to dead for Jax. They were parasites. Without a human to feed on, they would be dead.

"And these three bodies aren't dead, also?" Jax asked.

Vague memories of notes on vampyres were coming back to him. He remembered now that after turning someone, they had to be buried for a certain number of days. Jax had a feeling since the lawyer was hanging around that their earthen baking was almost complete.

Henry stared at the three mounds of dirt. "Two of them are dead, but my wife is not."

Jax raised an eyebrow at the older man. Sure it was dark out, and he wasn't completely clear to Jax in the dark of the night, but Jax was positive that Henry could see his face perfectly.

"I tried to turn my sons. They refused. Both of them. They would rather be dead than be a night human," Henry explained. "They won't be rising tonight, but my wife will. She wanted to spend a lifetime with me, and now we can. I regret that my sons couldn't see what a better life they would have, but I can't change that."

Jax nodded, but still felt the man was a little bit crazy. There was no way possible Jax would make someone become a monster of the night. He spent his life killing the ones that got out of line, but that didn't mean he liked the ones that kept their noses clean. He would kill almost all of them if he was allowed to. He had seen too many times how they could change too easily.

"Then why did you kill them if they didn't want to become one? Why not just leave them human?" Jax wondered out loud.

Henry stared at the piles of fresh dirt.

"I didn't know they wouldn't want to turn. I bled them nearly dry, and then they both told me no. There was nothing I could do to save them. I could turn them or let them die. I might be a monster, but I respected their choice. I'll have to live the rest of my long life knowing I did that to them." Henry felt some sort of remorse. Jax stared across the dark at the gray-haired man. He wished he could read his face better. Was it true remorse, or just something left over from being human? Most night humans lost that quality when they changed.

"And you're prepared to feed your wife once she wakes?" Jax asked. The man looked like he carried nothing, but easily could have packets of blood on him. Jax was pretty certain most night humans needed a lot of blood when they turned, but maybe vampyre took less blood.

"Feed? Sure, we're heading back into town tonight and will stop by one of the blood banks on the way," Henry replied, staring at one of the mounds of dirt.

Jax couldn't stop his eyes from bugging. Sure, he didn't remember the specifics on vampyres, but this man seemed to know even less. Why in the world would he turn someone with having so little knowledge?

"Weren't you turned just six months ago?" Jax asked. How could he know so little? And it seemed like his law office dealt with night humans in general. Shouldn't he know more?

"Yes, why?"

A hand popped out of the middle burial mound. Jax didn't hesitate to reach down and grab a stake from his boot. It seemed like Henry was right. Jax was never going to get away from night humans. Even if he wanted a normal life, it was like they would always find him. A second arm stretched out of the dirt and Henry reached forward. He had no clue what he had done, but Jax was ready to save himself when the new vampyre emerged with a lust for human blood that would dictate her every move. Jax was pretty sure he was the only human around, and more than positive the closest one. Life couldn't just be normal or boring.

Jax held his stake steady in his hand. He had to account for the fact that the newly turned were more savage and stronger than most night humans, but beyond that Jax was ready. That part wasn't going to be fun, and there was the added problem of the husband lurking around without the slightest clue what he was unleashing. Jax had to hope he would understand and let Jax put her down before she could kill anyone.

Henry didn't notice Jax's now defensive stance. He was smiling as the dirty woman emerged from the ground. She didn't look at her doting husband. Her head was now in the air, sniffing around. She was already searching for blood. Henry didn't even notice. The monster that had emerged from the ground could have been his wife, but only in body. Right now she was a very hungry, feral animal.

Jax had a gun hidden on himself also, but he was pretty sure in the dark he wasn't going to be his best shot. If he had been around for a few days, it would be easier to adjust to the dark. Jax had found the longer he stayed in an area, the better he adjusted to the nighttime darkness. He wasn't adjusted to Louisiana at all. But the gun would come in handy if she got close enough. He didn't have vampyre bullets loaded, but any creature would go down if hit enough times, and once down he could stake her. That was as long as the husband didn't step in. He'd have to deal with two then.

"Lori," Henry said, trying to get his wife's attention. She didn't turn to him. Her blood red eyes were still staring at Jax.

"His blood smells wrong," she finally said, pointing at Jax. "I'm hungry, and he doesn't smell like food. He smells like something different."

"Lori, don't worry about him. We'll head into town, and I'll get you some blood that smells much better." Henry reached for her hand. Lori didn't let him touch her as she took off into the woods.

Jax looked at the stunned lawyer. As far as he knew, it was miles to town. The new night human was either going to go feast on some nearby animal, or she was planning to run all the way back to town.

"Who's your closest neighbor?" Jax asked as he turned to run back to his bike. That would be the fastest way. Henry stood and stared into the darkness like she had slapped him on the way, but Jax knew she hadn't touched the vampyre, just as she hadn't made a move to attack him either. That was just another question to add to the mix.

"The Fullers live six miles south of here. They are the closest," Henry replied, still staring into the dark.

Jax didn't wait for the lawyer to get his head screwed back on right. He had to make sure the new night human didn't drain some innocent family on her way back to town. He had to hope she liked gator blood, but was pretty sure it was human blood she craved. Jax was lucky his unusual hunter strength seemed to double at night as he ran back to his waiting bike. He wasn't as fast as the vampyre, but he was pretty quick. Jax froze as he reached for his keys and looked at the house in front of him. There was someone that had to live closer.

"Where does Charlie live?" Jax asked Henry, who had followed him.

Henry's eyes went as large as saucers. Jax would have laughed if it was any other time. Night humans weren't usually as full of expression as the old lawyer. But then again, most night humans knew a lot more than the older man.

"He lives just down that path with his wife and child," Henry said, taking off in the direction he had pointed as he finally understood the gravity of the situation. Jax followed close behind.

The run wasn't far, but it was far enough, and they were too much behind. They weren't going to make it in time, even running at full speed. The slurping sound hit Jax before he came to the scene in the front of a rundown house. Someone was crumpled on the ground, and someone else was in the arms of the new night human Lori. Henry hurried over to his wife.

"Honey, leave her alone. You like Ella. Stop before you kill her."

Henry reached down to pull his wife off the body she was sucking the life from. Henry must not have gotten the memo on new night humans. She pushed him back with such force that he hit a tree ten feet away, leaving him slightly impaled on a sharp branch. Terror shot across his face as he realized that his wife wasn't who he thought she would be.

Jax didn't hesitate to go to the second person. Lori lifted her head and followed him with her eyes. Not turning back to her, Jax reached down and felt the man's neck. It was the same man Jax had met only hours before, and his pulse was still beating. Jax would have liked to throw Charlie into his house, but he wasn't sure if they had let the new vampyre in or not. Vampyre were the one kind of night human that was cursed with not being able to enter people's homes without permission. Jax always thought that was a funny curse, but every night human had a downfall and a strength. It was better to just keep himself between the night human and the unconscious man.

"I'm going to need you to stop feeding before you kill her," Jax said while he rolled back his sleeve. His hunter's mark, a Celtic cross, glowed in the dark. As it was exposed to the moonlight, more strength filled his body.

Screeching, Lori pulled back and covered her eyes. That was all the opening Jax needed as he jumped forward, faster than any normal human. He pushed the stake in his hand into the chest of the new night human. Jax tuned out the groan from the man impaled on the tree only feet away. Lori looked up at Jax as his stake pushed farther into her body. He needed to hit the heart to kill her. She finally realized what was going on and lashed out at him with her sharp nails. She caught the flesh of his arm, but was too late to stop him as she crumbled to ash.

Jax didn't pause to look at the mess he made. He instead went over to the man that was slowly regaining consciousness. Jax pulled him up to standing and helped him toward the open door. Peeking out of the corner of the window was a small child.

"Did you give Henry permission to come in your house in

the past six months?" Jax asked. Charlie looked at Jax in confusion. "Henry Lawrence?" Jax pointed back at the tree where the vampyre was trying to pull himself off.

"Henry? What is going on? Henry's been dead for longer than that." Charlie turned to go back to the man he had worked for his whole life.

"Get inside your house. I'll deal with this," Jax ordered him. Charlie looked like he was going to argue, but Jax just shoved him inside. Charlie stumbled and ended up on the floor. "Make sure he stays inside the house," Jax told the child that had to be at least six or seven years old.

Jax walked back to Henry.

"You do understand this is your fault?" Jax asked, staring at the man that hadn't worked himself off the tree branch yet.

"You killed her," Henry said like he was in shock. Not what Jax had expected. Anger was the most likely feeling he'd have expected from killing someone a night human loved, but Henry wasn't angry.

"When a night human turns, they need blood. They can't wait for a stroll into town. They eat the first human they find and drain them. It isn't a casual feeding. They need a lot of blood," Jax explained. Henry's eyes widened for a second time that night. "I can check, but I'm pretty sure she killed that lady. She would have also killed Charlie and the kid, too, if I hadn't stopped her."

"She murdered Ella?" Henry finally spoke, looking at the crumpled human woman on the ground. "But I didn't kill anyone when I was turned. That's not what I've seen at all. Why did she do that?"

"I don't know why you didn't kill anyone, but it's normal for night humans to kill. Didn't your master explain all this to you when you asked to turn her?"

Henry stared up at Jax. The look told him everything. Jax could see it in his eyes. Henry hadn't asked for permission. Jax reached forward and yanked the older man off the tree.

Henry knew nothing of the night human world, even if he now was one. He probably didn't even know the rules to being the kind he was. All night humans had rules, and Henry would need to learn them quickly.

"Do you have permission to enter their house?" Jax asked, getting back on task. He kind of felt sorry for the older man, but even so, Jax felt stronger the need to protect the defenseless day humans.

"Permission?" Henry was still confused.

Grasping the older man's shirt, Jax pulled him to the doorway. As Jax walked into the house with Henry, the man ran into an invisible wall.

"Good enough for me," Jax said as he walked back out to the man now rubbing his hurt face. Jax hadn't been too gentle about it.

"I don't understand," Henry added. He was genuinely confused still.

"Your wife was crazy with blood lust. She must have attacked this one outside the house." Jax pointed to the crumpled form of the lady. "She also must have knocked Charlie out to feed on him later." The whole situation made sense to Jax, but he had been around night humans his whole life. For someone new to the night human world it would be confusing, but that is why Henry should have been taught.

"But my wife was a pacifist. She's never raised a hand to a fly." Henry was still in shock as he now stared at the pile of ashes on the ground. "Where did she go?"

"Pacifist or not, she was hungry. I don't know what rock you've been hiding under, but this is the night human world and everything that I want to get away from. All this death." Jax motioned to the dead woman on the front porch of the house.

Looking at the dead lady seemed to bring back more humanity to Henry.

"Should we call someone?"

It was Jax's turn to stare at the man in disbelief.

"You need to take care of this like you did your sons. If you didn't have permission from your master to turn your wife, it was your responsibility to keep her from killing. You'll be punished for it. Clean up after yourself."

Jax hated to have to act like the parent, but this guy was in need of it. It was obvious he knew nothing of the real night human world, and since Jax still didn't have his answer, he needed the man alive for the time being. He'd help him survive, at least for now.

"I'll stay here all night with Charlie and explain things to him in the morning. You can take care of this mess and get back to wherever your nest is before someone comes looking," Jax explained. "Who does the deed of your house go to if you and your family dies?"

"Charlie," Henry replied as he stared into the house. "Will he be okay?"

"Physically? Yes." Jax glanced at the man on the couch now. Somehow the kid had gotten his father onto the couch and tucked him in. "Mentally? That will take a bit to adjust to. No one takes hearing about night humans well. I'll make sure he is fine. For now, just know that you can never come back home. It is his home now, and that means you aren't invited in."

Henry nodded and moved to pick up the dead lady. He glanced down again at the piles of his wife's clothing, now covered in dust. He seemed to still be in shock.

"Your father's name is Wes," Henry said as he walked away.

Jax nodded at his back as Henry left. That was one step closer. After dealing with the humans that knew nothing of the horrible world of the night, Jax would go back to his hotel room and finally get some answers. Henry might not have noticed, but he had given Jax his father's full name on accident when he'd called him Jaxton Cunningham. Wes Cunningham was who Jax was looking for. He might get some answers before he turned eighteen after all.

CHAPTER 5

After spending the night with Charlie and his son, Jax was happy to make it back to his hotel room. He couldn't wait to crash and get some much-needed sleep. The child would not sleep unless Jax was awake. He even woke a few times to check on Jax, and Jax was pretty sure he wouldn't be able to sleep anyways. He couldn't be too sure who Charlie had let into his house or not. It was typically stressful to explain night humans to people, but it turned out to be much easier after they had seen one.

Jax climbed the stairs instead of using the elevator and made it the three floors to the hallway that led to his room without incident. It was nice to not find any night humans hanging about his hotel. He was completely ready to have a night human free hour or two. With the sun fully out, he knew he was safe to move around with no night humans following. He found himself wishing for a boring, night human free life yet again.

Turning the corner to his room, Jax wasn't actually surprised to find Jen standing there waiting. She smiled at him as he noticed her and pushed herself off the wall she had been leaning against. Jax pushed past her and opened his room door. He walked in, but blocked her from following.

"I don't want anything to do with your uncle or the night humans he works with," Jax said as he snapped back around to find himself face-to-face with the teenager.

She stared up at him, not afraid in the least at his hostile tone. "I want nothing to do with them either, but family is family. You can't change who you're related to," Jen replied stubbornly.

"Fair enough, but go away. If I deal with you, then I'm

dealing with them. Really, nothing against you, but I have enough to figure out on my own." Jax didn't mind being blunt. He didn't have time to wait around and play games. His mother could show up at any time and force him home. In fact, he was surprised she hadn't done it yet. He still had his role to play for the hunters, and he was pretty sure she'd already made all his life decisions for him.

"What if I could help you figure things out?" she asked.

Jax just stared at her with his "get out of here" face. It had no effect on her. Jax needed to work harder on that, or maybe Jen was immune to it if she dealt with night humans all the time. They were normally way scarier than Jax could be, or maybe it just wasn't working because he was sleep deprived.

"Not needed. I'm doing fine on my own," Jax replied.

Actually, he had a few lucky breaks, but he wasn't about to tell her that. Her uncle and his folder would be the easiest way to get his answers, but he was serious that he wasn't going to deal with them and whoever he was associated with.

"Come on. I know your answers are slow coming, and I have access to my uncle's law firm. They let me wander around that place all the time. I could be a big help to you, and you know it. Just let me prove it to you. Give me a chance."

Jen obviously wasn't too proud to beg. Jax moved to shut the door in her face, but she stepped closer, putting herself within inches of him. She tilted her head up, making her ponytail swing down behind her. One tug and she would tip backward, out of his way, but there was something about her that made him not do it. Maybe it was the desperation in her eyes, or because she looked very much like Jade, but he didn't.

"If you're offering, then you want something in return," Jax deduced.

She was desperate, but he just didn't know what he could offer the girl. She didn't need protection. The night humans worked with her uncle. There's no way they would hurt her. He really had no clue what he could offer.

"I know you're a hunter. I knew the first moment I saw you come into town. I want you to train me on how to fight." Jen looked at him like she was waiting for his surprise.

Surprise wasn't coming from Jax. That was probably the only thing he had that she could want, and it made complete sense. He didn't need to sort out if she was lying. He trusted she was telling the truth on that one.

"My parents are dead, and no one will tell me why or how they died. That only adds up to one thing in this town, and that's night humans. I want to be able to protect myself from them, and you're my best bet for learning how. I went and found out the name of the guy who is sending you the money. I can help you, and you can help me."

Jax shook his head as she stepped back. He wasn't about to move. It was all good that she wanted him to teach her how to fight, and yes that was the one thing he could do, but that didn't mean he was going to do it. He had a limited time to find answers, and he couldn't spend it on training some teenager. She was now farther out in the hallway and waiting for his reply. Jax pushed the door closed before she could stop him and clicked the bolt into place.

Jen pounded on the locked door.

"Jax, come on. I can help you. Don't you want to know the name of the guy sending you money?" Jen could be heard through the door.

"Wes Cunningham," Jax told her.

Silence came from the doorway and Jax opened it back up. Jen stared at him in disbelief. That was the only card she held to bargain with.

"Wes Cunningham," Jax repeated as he looked at her.

Her defeated face was pulled into a frown. Jax actually felt bad for her. From what he could guess, she must have only been a few years younger than him. He could tell there had to be some reason she wanted to learn how to fight, but

Jax wasn't about to pull any innocent people into the mix. He was already dealing with night humans when he didn't want to. He knew what a human girl was to night humans: *dinner*. They wouldn't hesitate for a second to hurt her if they knew she was associated with him. In fact, her parents association with her uncle could be the reason they weren't around. That was the likely scenario when dealing with leeches.

"What if I get you the folder?" Jen asked as her disappointment turned into determination.

Jax gave her his best "I doubt you're capable" look.

"I can. I know where my uncle keeps everything. I can get you the folder, and then you don't have to run around cemeteries to find more information," Jen quickly added. She had to be following him. She was pretty good at it, too, as Jax hadn't noticed her at the mausoleum. Then again, his senses were more attuned to night humans than day humans.

"Don't get involved. The folder is locked away in a safe deposit box. You won't find it in your uncle's office," Jax told her. "And learning how to fight isn't a one-time thing. I can fight night humans because I've been training to do it since I could walk. This has been my whole life. One lesson won't make you a pro."

"I understand that." Jen pouted and made Jax miss Jade even more. His sister would use that same exact look every time she wanted to get her way. "All I'm asking for is like one hour a day of your time. Tell me how to get stronger, show me how. Teach me how to train when you leave. That's all I ask. I know perfectly well what night humans are like, and I know what my uncle deals with. If he makes one wrong choice, it's me that will pay the consequences. Show me how to defend myself. I'm desperate. I'll do anything for you. I'll get that folder you say is impossible to get. Anything."

Jax wanted to tell her no. He wanted to keep her away from all the night humans and the night human world he no longer desired to be a part of himself. She had a choice to get out, and he was never going to have that option. But she was right. With her uncle working with them, there was no way she was getting out of it until she could run off on her own and disappear. Even then she could still be a target, after giving up her whole life. Training her was probably the best option.

"Fine. If you will help me get that folder, I promise to spend one hour a day training you. Now, I suggest you also start running a few miles every morning when you get up and do some weight training because, otherwise, you'll never be able to keep up with me."

Jumping forward, Jen hugged Jax. He laughed at her enthusiasm. She wasn't going to be as happy with him after her first training session since he wasn't planning to go easy on her. If she really wanted to learn, she would put up with it. If not, he had one more hour to get his own research done.

"Thank you, thank you, thank you," she said into his chest. "I promise I'll get that file. I'll search his whole office top to bottom to find the safe deposit key or code or whatever. You won't be disappointed in me. I promise."

"Fine. Now let me get some sleep, and I'll see you tomorrow at noon to begin training."

Jen hugged him one more time and then ran off down the hallway. It was like he had just told her she had won the lottery. Jax shook his head as he shut the door. She didn't have the slightest clue what she was getting into, but she would find out … after he got some sleep.

Jax took the few steps to the bed and flopped down, tossing his shirt off on the way and going to sleep the moment he shut his eyes.

Jax woke sometime in the night. He was sure he hadn't slept too much, but killing a night human was always exhausting and led to troubled dreams. Sure, they were blood suckers that killed normal people, but at the same time, they had also been people once. Part of him wanted to call his sister and brag that he could kill them on his own, but he knew better. If he told Jade anything about the vampyre being around, or him killing one because it had attacked and killed a human, they would send a team to town. He would no longer get to continue his search for answers, and they would likely force him home since the whole world still saw him as a minor.

It was still early enough in the afternoon that Jax had plenty of time to search for information on his father, Wes Cunningham, before Jen would come around to train. A name was a great start, but he wanted to know as much as he could about the man. He was family, after all, and the only family his mother never talked about, which made Jax want to know more.

Starting with basic searches, he was surprised to find there was very little about anyone named Wes Cunningham in New Orleans, or Louisiana for that matter. Jax did find a corporation owned by a Wes Cunningham, but no pictures beyond a very fuzzy, grainy one. It wasn't going to be good enough to convince him that the man was his father if he couldn't see what he even looked like.

Jen arrived early, and Jax was still perusing the web pages. He had found the name mentioned, but he was still not finding a single good picture.

"Did you try typing in his full name?" Jen asked as she ate a donut behind him, peering over his shoulder at the computer screen.

"Full name? I'm pretty sure Wes Cunningham is his full name, unless you have a middle name to look for also."

Jax didn't mean to be snippy, but he was frustrated. Every time it felt like he was getting close, there was another hurdle in the way. He just wanted to know who the man was and why he was sending him money. Why was it that he never met the man before if he knew where he lived? Did his father want no contact? Why send the money then? It made no sense. Either the man wanted to know Jax, or he didn't. But it seemed like both at once.

"Isn't Wes short for Wesley?" Jen asked.

Jax wanted to hit his head on the desk. *Why didn't I think of that?* It made complete sense. Wes was a nickname. He searched again, but found Wesley Cunningham and Louisiana had about as much traction as Wes did. There was only one page he could find that was relevant, and it really wasn't. It was about a plantation owner named Wesley Cunningham from the 1800's. All he learned was that Wes was a family name. That page again didn't have a picture, which would have been nice.

"Did you find the article on Pearly Meds?" Jen asked. Obviously, she had been researching also. While he didn't want to involve her, it seemed like she was willing to put herself right in the middle of everything regardless.

"Yeah. All they had was a bunch of stuff about him taking over for his father," Jax replied as he continued to look at the plantation article.

"Go back to the Meds one," Jen ordered.

Jax glared at the bossy girl behind him. Jen flashed him a bright smile and pushed his rolling chair over as she began to type away at his computer. Soon enough she had opened the business page that had the name Wes Cunningham. She began to scroll through the various pages of the business before stopping at picture of a group of people.

"Look. There are five names listed below but six people. I think that one of them is Wes," Jen explained.

Jax stared at the picture. All the men in the picture were in their thirties to forties. None of them looked like father material, and worse than that, they would have been very young when he was conceived. He knew his mother was barely twenty when he was born, but he always assumed his father was older than that.

"If we compare the business employee page to this one ..."

Jen began clicking open windows and comparing men to the picture. In under two minutes, she had five pages pulled up with the various men on them. Jax was boggled by the speed in which she found them. Jen shrugged.

"What can I say? Computers are a hobby of mine. Anyway, these five guys all still work for the place, so that only leaves this one." Jen pointed at the youngest man in the group. There was no way that he could be his father.

"When the article said Wes was young, I was thinking they meant he was young to be running a business, not that he was barely older than me," Jax said as he stared at the man in the picture. He couldn't have been much more than twenty, with dark hair that perfectly matched Jax's, and the nose that all but proved they were related.

"I figured this was the guy in the article, but I didn't know you'd think that it was your father. I'm assuming with a family name that this is your older brother," Jen explained rationally.

What she was thinking made sense. Wesley seemed to be a family name, and Jax's older brother would be named that instead of him. And just looking at the guy, Jax knew he was family. He had the same face shape as Jade. Now he wondered why his older brother took over the business. Was their father still alive? Jax was possibly looking for answers where there weren't any, at least online.

Jax hated how complicated his life was. Killing night humans had been easier than having to deal with the questions he had now. Every answer led to ten more questions. Now he needed to figure out who this older brother was and what that meant also. Jax hadn't even thought about having more family. He had been searching for his father and not considering that there would be more to go with it. It made sense, though. Jax did have Jade. It was more than possible that their father had more children. Now

Jax wondered if it was his father sending money, or the brother since they had the same name?

"I did stop by my uncle's place this morning. They are closed on Tuesdays." Jen moved over and let Jax look more at the photo. "I didn't find the folder at all, as we expected, and there was nothing about a safe deposit box. I'm guessing I'll have to check at home when he's at work. But what I did find might be more helpful."

Jen stepped back to the bed and the duffle bag she had brought with. Digging inside, she pulled out an envelope and handed it to Jax.

"My uncle was cordially invited to a nice party, and I figured we could go snoop around if you'd like." Jen shrugged like she wasn't sure if Jax would want to go or not.

Jax opened the envelope. Inside was a fancy invitation to a party as Jen had described, but he hadn't missed who was throwing it: Wes Cunningham.

"Seems my uncle does business with him, but didn't plan to attend. I asked him this morning if I could go since I love all these parties that he's invited to and he told me only if I brought a date. He doesn't like me to go alone, but he doesn't care if I go." Jen shrugged. Her uncle seemed to not care if she was in danger. Then again, he did business with night humans. He wasn't placing her safety on any level of priority. Teaching her to fight was probably her best option.

"This is nice and all, but I don't exactly have a suit with me." Jax pointed to the writing that described it as a black tie event.

Jen grinned. "I took care of everything. There's a suit in here. I had to guess your size. I also brought a dress for me, and I took one of my uncle's cars. I had a feeling this was a good lead."

Jax shook his head. "Why didn't you lead with that conversation?" She'd been sitting in his room eating breakfast and helping him look over the Internet for over an hour.

Jen shrugged. "I wasn't sure if you'd believe who the guy was if I explained it was your brother. When I found the picture last night, I recognized him. I knew my uncle has done business with him and that he was invited to this party tonight. It seemed like a perfect set up, but I wanted you to see with your own eyes that this man wasn't your father that you would be meeting."

While Jen seemed trustworthy, Jax was sure she was still hiding something. He felt she was genuine in wanting to learn how to fight and help him, but he wasn't sure of the reason why. Jax stood up and turned off his computer. Jen had some sort of secret, and Jax had to hope it wasn't the kind that would get them in trouble.

"Fine. After the workout, we can go to the party. And next time, just give me the facts. I doubt there's anything you could say that I'll automatically think is a lie. I've grown up in the night human world and everything there is unbelievable to outsiders. Trust me. I believe in weird coincidences more than most."

Jax might have been a bit tougher on Jen than he'd intended in their training session. Maybe he was trying to prove a point—that it wasn't a one-time thing that would keep her safe—or maybe he was just having fun. It had been months since Jade had joined him for a workout and it was nice to have someone to talk to, or in Jen's case, grunt back at. He took her through a full session, even though she barely made it through the last twenty minutes. Jax was refreshed and able to work hard, even doubling all the counts that Jen did because he had enough pent up energy to do twice the amount of work than her.

Even though Jen was exhausted, she didn't protest once. Best of all, she didn't complain when they trudged back upstairs from the exercise room in the hotel to his room to get ready for the party, and he made them climb the stairs. Jax wasn't opposed to elevators, but he didn't see the point of all the standing around for three flights of stairs. He wouldn't be winded if he ran up them. Jen was winded before she took the first step. She had a long way to go to be strong enough to defend herself, but it was a start.

Jax let Jen shower first as he knew girls and how long it took them to get ready to go to a party. After he'd cleaned up, he was surprised to find that Jen had guessed exactly right on his sizes. The three-piece suit she brought with fit him perfectly. Jax was ready to go and waited for Jen to finish with her make-up and hair. Surprisingly, she was quicker than Jade used to be as Jen came out in a red sparkly dress with a slit that went past her fingertips. Jade was never one for long dresses, but the slit would make it able for Jen to move around freely if they encountered anything they needed to run from, he noted. Jax just couldn't turn off the hunter inside him.

"You don't look too bad all cleaned up," Jen commented.

Jax just grunted. It wasn't his favorite thing, to wear a suit. He had on more than one occasion, but he did find them restrictive. One good thing was they hid his weapons well. Jax went over to his stash and began to pick out a few. Strapping a few stakes on his legs under the pants and tucking his favorite pistol away in the gun holster under his coat was enough to keep him feeling safe.

Jen just stared at him with an open mouth. "I thought we were just going to look for information ..."

"And while doing that, what do we do if we run into night humans? Tell them we are just snooping, no need to eat us?"

Jen seemed confused. Jax just laughed.

"Let's just say that I seem to attract night humans. And I was raised to never go anywhere without at least two weapons. Five might be a little excessive, but I'm finding this city is more filled with the leeches than anyone knows."

"Five?"

Jax smiled and didn't elaborate. Yes, she was now his ally, but he wasn't about to tell her where all his weapons were hidden. The art of surprise was one of the best ways to fight a night human. They all fought the same. They depended on their strength with whatever trick their clan could do. Every night human race had a different specialty. They relied heavily on that one trick. None of them expected day humans to fight back, and that was always the best way to win a fight he didn't want to start in the first place.

"Now, if we could get going, I'd love to get there before sunset," Jax told Jen. "It works better to get the layout and find alternative ways to leave a place. And to do it in the sunlight when they aren't watching."

Jen held up the keys to a car for Jax. He took them from her.

"You sound like you plan to find trouble," Jen added as she led the way out of the hotel room.

After grabbing his smaller duffle bag, Jax followed behind her.

"Trouble is everywhere. I don't expect to find it, but I do expect to not be caught off guard. There's nothing worse than pretending life is fine when it isn't. That's why most people get caught and become food for night humans; they don't think it'll happen to them."

Jen led the way back down to the parked car. Luckily for Jax, she kept quiet the whole way as the GPS led them to the mansion they were going to. Jax appreciated the silence and stayed in his own thoughts. He kept his guard up and memorized everything on the drive there. Jen just watched him as he did so. When they reached the house, the valet offered to take and park the car. Jax wanted to refuse. Knowing where their getaway vehicle was could be critical.

"You want to control everything, I get it, but let this one go. If you make a scene, then you don't blend in. Getting information and following people is my specialty. We'll be able to snoop around easier if you don't make a scene," Jen quickly whispered before smiling up at the man opening her door. She handed him her invitation.

Jen had him there. They did need to blend in, and Jax certainly didn't want to draw any attention to them before they even entered the house. He didn't have a quick reply, and there was no time left to argue. Jax stepped out of the car as the valet came over to his door. Jen waited for him on the steps of the house. Taking her arm, Jax led Jen inside.

Surprisingly, the party was already in full swing despite the sun not setting yet. People were scattered all over the house, mingling and talking in small groups. Jax's night human senses were going off full blast, and he tried his best not to crane his neck around every time they passed another night human. It seemed they didn't wait until sunset to come out to this party. That alone made Jax want to look around more. Something was strange about the Cunningham house and the night humans lingering around.

"Still not fitting in," Jen whispered to Jax as they made their way to a large open space that was dotted with standing tables and trays of hors d'ourves on one side of the room.

"I fit in a lot better when I don't feel like my life is threatened," Jax replied under his breath. He was sure several of them would hear what he said, and he couldn't be more open about it. He wanted to point out each and every leech in the room to Jen to get her to understand how many were wandering around.

Jen smiled and laughed a little. "My uncle doesn't mind that we came in place of him. This whole thing isn't his scene anyway."

She didn't get his meaning. Jen leaned in and patted the arm she was holding with her other hand.

"Are you thirsty? I think I'll go get something for us to drink."

And like that she was off into the mass of people lounging around the room. It was a crowd that included at least fifteen night humans. Jax watched Jen as she weaved her way between people, stopping every so often to say hello. She did know many of them. None of the night humans were on her list of visiting, though. He wasn't sure if that was because she really didn't know them, or because she didn't want Jax to know she knew them. She didn't seem worried in the least.

Jax felt the phone in his pocket vibrate and he pulled it out. Jen had left him a message.

The majority of vampyre stay in this main room. They will be watching the women the most, so you have the best chance to sneak around to find out more.

So she did know after all. That still wasn't comforting. Most of the vampyre he saw in the room were male. Jen would be a perfect target, and he didn't feel safe leaving her alone. As Jax looked around the room, the male night humans were mainly watching the women while the few female night humans were already hanging on the arms of men twice their age. Jen seemed to be right about them being more male and him not being a target. Jax spotted a staircase on the far side of the room. It would give him a better view to make sure Jen was safe before he wandered off to see what he could find.

Jax climbed the stairs and stopped at the top. He had a great view of the room from the balcony overlooking the large room. Jen was down toward the food and drinks, talking to someone. She didn't seem to notice he was gone and it was a perfect opportunity to just watch. The man with her was a normal human, but like the vampyre ladies, he was older than Jen. He was talking to her, and she was smiling. When she said she went to the parties a lot, it seemed like it was true. Was she a night human sympathizer? It would put a kink in his plans if she were just using him. But Jax didn't think it was that. Something else was her secret.

"Enjoying the party?"

Jax didn't turn to the man beside him. It was a night

human, and probably the one left upstairs to keep guests from wandering the rest of the house. Jax wasn't going to get further that way, but there was always the downstairs.

"Parties aren't my sort of thing," Jax replied, finally turning to the man beside him.

"Neither for me, but what can I do? When you own a company, you are expected to do certain things like throwing parties for employees and investors."

Jax didn't need to be introduced to the guy to understand he was standing next to Wes Cunningham. His own brother was right there beside him. Jax tried not to stare and quickly looked back down at the people mingling around. He knew there would be questions if he openly stared at the man.

"I wouldn't know. I only own my bike, and that doesn't require entertainment."

Wes laughed. "Some days I wish that was my life. This suit stuff and pretending to be something you're not grows boring after a while. A bike and the open road sounds just about perfect to me."

"Mr. Cunningham," someone called from the base of the stairs.

"Thanks for coming. Enjoy the party," Wes said as he walked past Jax. "Wait. I forget my manners. I didn't introduce myself. I'm Wes Cunningham." The man offered his hand to Jax.

Jax took the extended hand. A jolt shot through his arm, and he tried his best to pretend nothing happened. He knew exactly who the man was, but in typical Jax fashion, it just led to him having more questions than answers.

"Jax Kristian," Jax replied as he looked the guy in the eyes.

Wes stared back with a giant smile.

"Make yourself at home, Jax."

Jax nodded to Wes before he turned and walked down the stairs to the waiting man. Jax followed Wes's movement across the room with his gaze. He stopped almost as often as

Jen to talk to people before eventually making it to the far side of the room. Jax didn't wait to see why the man was walking to the microphone set up as he skipped down the stairs two at a time. Jen was close enough for him to grab her and leave.

"Where are we going?" Jen whispered as Jax pulled her back toward the front door. She was glancing at the hallways as they passed a few that were guarded by vampyres.

"Out of here, now," Jax replied. He could take on a few night humans, but over a dozen and one more powerful than he had ever met wasn't an option. He needed to rethink everything, and it was best to do that back in the safety of his hotel room.

"Wait," Jen resisted, trying to pull them to a stop.

"No waiting. We need to leave now," Jax told her. Jen went to complain again, and Jax turned to glare at her. "You can make this easy or hard, but we're leaving now."

She heard the anger in his voice and stopped protesting. Jax was thankful. His mind was already swimming, and he didn't need dealing with a teenage girl that didn't want to leave a party to the list. It wasn't often that Jax was surprised. He should have known that the party was too easy of a solution. Heck, he should have known something was up with all the night humans hanging around. He hadn't thought about what it could mean, and it caught him off guard. He needed to think it all over and figure it out some place safe.

His older brother was a night human.

CHAPTER 6

Jax **pulled out** of the Cunningham driveway and didn't give a second glance back in case Jen was watching him, which she was. He didn't need to look back to know it wasn't good. There was a silver car following them, but Jen didn't seem to notice. She was still glaring at him for leaving the party. It was almost like she wanted to be at the party for more than just digging on information for him.

"We have another piece of the puzzle," Jax said casually, while still watching the gray car swerve between lanes on the highway to stay near them. Jax had to make a plan, and quickly.

"You didn't go snooping. I was keeping attention on me and giving you the opportunity to go off and look around. You never left the room. Didn't you want to learn more about your brother and possibly your guy's father?"

"I didn't need to snoop once I met Wes Cunningham," Jax replied as he changed all three lanes at once and watched the car not too far back do the same. He might have been paranoid and seeing things, but as he moved around on the highway, he was certain they were being followed.

"You met Mr. Cunningham himself? He's like magic at these things. He appears from nowhere and disappears before anyone can talk to him. Did you tell him you're his brother?"

"No. I gave him my name, but didn't say that we're related. The more I think about it, I'm second guessing that he's my brother," Jax explained as he moved back the three lanes to watch the car following do the same. It was not looking good. Jax wanted to think they were just thugs following them and that he could take them, but he didn't want to confront a car full of night humans with Jen there. She easily could be hurt in any fight.

"Not your brother? How is that possible? You guys look alike, and we know he's the one sending you money. It makes sense. Did you not see that place? That family is loaded." Jen continued to talk. She still hadn't noticed their latest problem.

"I'm not saying he's not related. I'm saying I have to go digging more into it tomorrow since Wes Cunningham happens to be a vampyre."

Jax whipped the car around and drove off the highway the wrong direction onto the on-ramp leading to the highway. The car tailing them wasn't expecting him to do that, and it only worked because being late at night there weren't as many cars around. He didn't need to dodge any oncoming traffic and had picked the perfect ramp to leave the highway from. Jax had waited until the highway was getting light on traffic and luck was on his side with no one coming on to the ramp.

"What the heck are you doing?" Jen screeched as she was slammed into the door and finally noticed his abnormal driving. It was funny that she never complained about his three lane sweeps he was doing across the highway as they talked.

"Losing our tail, which I expect are night humans." Jax pulled off the road and quickly sped away. The silver car was surprised by his action, but that didn't mean they wouldn't follow.

"What do you mean we're being followed?" Jen was now looking behind them for the car. It still wasn't close enough to see Jax pull off the street into a parking ramp. She wouldn't find it, at least not yet.

Had Jax been alone, he wouldn't mind taking out his frustration on the unlucky night humans who dared to follow him, but since Jen was with him, Jax was taking the high road and keeping her safe. And if it was Wes, Jax really didn't want to deal with that either. His father or brother or whatever the man was to him was different than anyone Jax had met before. He seemed dangerous. Jax wasn't sure he could take on that much power if it came to a fight, but he wasn't about to tell Jen that.

Jax ripped out a ticket and pulled up the ramp of a random parking garage. It was nice that the parking garage was more than half full. It would make hiding easier. Jax drove up to the next level before turning to go back down toward the exit. Finding an area with several cars, he backed into a spot. *This will have to do*. The nice thing about the borrowed car was that the license plate was only on the back. If the people following knew what his car plates were, they wouldn't see it.

"Grab the middle of the seat and pull it down. You should be able to climb into the trunk from there," Jax directed Jen. She stared at him. "And you should do it quickly since I don't know how long before they follow us into the garage to look for the car."

"No way. You seriously want me to climb into the trunk?"

"Yes. It's the safest spot for you to be in case they do find us," Jax replied, exasperated in that all he wanted to do was keep her safe, and she was fighting him on it. "I think I have the car hidden, but that doesn't mean they won't find us. If you're in the trunk, they'll think I already dropped you off. If they're looking for you, then they'll leave me alone, and you'll be safe. If they're looking for me, then I'll deal with them without having to worry that you'll be in the way. Either way, you in the trunk is the best solution."

Jax stared at her in the dark garage. He could see her face perfectly and had a feeling she could see him, too. She huffed a few more times and then hiked her sparkly, ankle-length skirt up and climbed into the backseat. As expected, the seat pulled down, and she could climb into the trunk.

Jen turned back to him. "This isn't just a way to lock me

in the trunk, is it?"

Jax shook his head. "If I wanted to lock you in the trunk, I wouldn't be putting you in one with a safety latch that you could let yourself out at any time. Just get in there."

Jen looked like she was going to complain, but a car went by the opposite side of the garage on the up ramp. Jax couldn't see if it was the same car or not, but he didn't want to take any chances. Glancing back to Jen, he saw she had seen it, too. Quickly enough she scooted into the trunk and pulled the seat closed.

Jax pushed the driver's seat as far back as it would go and laid down to wait. The doors were locked, but that didn't make a difference to a night human. They had superhuman strength. Jax had the keys still in the ignition, and he flipped on the radio to a station that didn't quite come in. He had to hope the white noise would muffle his heartbeat if they were looking for him that way. He lay back with his hand on his gun. Sure, night humans were hard to kill with a bullet, but it knocked them down long enough for him to do something more. He had never understood why night humans didn't fight with guns, but he wasn't beyond using them. It was their loss to not have another way to fight, and he was trained well enough it was an asset in any situation.

The car that went up the other side was now coming down. Jax kept his window cracked open to listen as the car turned the corner to the level where they were parked. It was slowing down as it neared the group of cars where they were parked. Jax kept his breathing as steady and quiet as he could. He was glad Jen had listened to him and was in the trunk. He was certain she would have been freaking out.

As the silver car neared where Jax was parked, he could make out voices.

"Do you see it here?" a male voice asked.

"No. No black cars here," the second male voice replied.

Jax held his breath as they came closer.

"And no one that I can hear hiding around here either.

The hunter and the chick aren't here," the second voice added. They were listening for him, and the radio seemed to be doing the trick.

The silver car kept rolling by. Jax didn't remove his hand from his gun. They could just be trying to fool him. It seemed that even with his mark covered, the town knew he was a hunter. He needed to find out how and fix that if he ever went on a road trip again. Jax lay in his seat and listened as the car left. The gate to the garage opened with a ding, and the car sped away.

Jax remained in his spot and waited longer. He had plenty of patience and knew that acting too quickly was exactly what night humans counted on from day humans. Jax wasn't going to do that. Traffic passed on the road outside the garage, and Jax could hear that, too. He listened for anyone walking by. There was no one. Closing his eyes, Jax sensed for night humans. There was no one within the garage either, though he did feel someone passing outside. That was enough for Jax to know he would be spending his night in the car. He wasn't about to chance leaving and someone catching them on their way out. It would be better to wait until the sun rose to leave.

Slowly sitting up, Jax looked around the garage. There were only a few cars parked by him, but what he saw made him smile. He had thought the car he was driving was black also, but he didn't notice in the light of the garage the dark color was actually a blue. The car was navy, and no one would notice except that he happened to have parked next to a black truck that made his car look even bluer. Luck was on his side.

Reaching back, Jax pulled the middle seat down.

"They left, but I don't think we should take any chances. They only lost us because I pulled that u-ey on the highway. They'll know I know how to drive now and tricks like that won't work a second time. We'd do best to stay here until sunrise."

"Who were those guys?" Jen asked as she looked out from her space, but she didn't climb completely out.

"I don't know. Just one more mystery I guess."

"But something you're used to ..." Jen let it hang out there.

Jax was likely the target for his job alone. There were more than a few night humans that would like to get their hands on a hunter. And a large percentage of them would probably do about anything to get the child of Rommy. His mother had made many enemies over the years. It was likely that the night humans were after him. But there was also the chance that they were after Jen. Her uncle was dealing with night humans heavily. Jax had no clue what he was in to, and he really didn't want to know. Either one of them could have been the target, but Jax didn't want to stop and ask them why. It was really just another question to his ever-growing list.

"So back to what you said before. Wes Cunningham is a night human?"

"Yeah. Nice surprise of the night. My one clue turns out to be exactly what I don't want to deal with. I think that's called irony." Jax leaned back in his seat again, his head now closer to Jen. She remained in the trunk, but was still talking to him from there. The night had taken a very ironic turn after all.

"And if he's a night human, you don't know if he's your brother or father," Jen said as she figured out what was bothering him.

That was exactly what Jax had been pondering since he touched Wes. He wanted to try normal, but every time he thought he was getting away from the night human world, it pulled him back in. He really didn't want to learn more about Wes Cunningham now that he knew what he was. Although there was still the money, and what it meant. He was going to have to talk with Wes if he wanted to question him. Finding the answer would mean dealing with the night human that he was somehow related to. Life was more than ironic for Jax.

"Get some rest," Jax told her. "I'll keep us safe."

Jen yawned. She looked like she was going to protest, but decided otherwise. Jax was happy she was just going to agree for once, but it was possible that she didn't have the strength to protest. He had worked her hard with training, and it was probably past her bedtime as it was. She needed rest being a day human and all, and the car was the only place they'd be getting it.

Jax glanced back at Jen. She had already closed her eyes. He smiled. Her sleeping face appeared less mature than her awake face, and he could tell she had to be years younger than him no matter how tough she talked or acted. She didn't need to be in the night human world. He wanted to find a way to keep her out of it so that she could have a normal life, one that he was beginning to see she was never going to get.

"**I don't care**," Jen replied as she sat in the front seat of the car. She had changed into a T-shirt, but refused to go back to her uncle's place. She was well rested after sleeping in the car and ready to give Jax a hard time.

"Just go home," Jax begged. He was tired. She might have slept soundly, but he didn't sleep a wink keeping them safe. Jax needed at least a couple hours' worth of a nap before he could figure out what to do.

"I'm not going back there. What if the people last night were looking for me? They could be waiting at my uncle's place. I don't feel safe. I'm not going back there. You can't make me."

Jax stood with his hand on the knob of his hotel room door. He wasn't about to sleep with her sitting in the room wide awake. He trusted her only a tad bit more than a stranger, and that wasn't saying much. Jax tended to view everyone as an enemy until he shook their hand and found out if they were a night human or not. She wasn't a night human, but she did have a secret she was keeping from him. That meant he wasn't going to completely trust her.

"Go back to your uncle's place, and we can meet later to work out. I'm in no condition to go for a run at the moment."

Jen glared at him. That wasn't what she wanted at all, even if Jax pretended that was the case.

"I'm not leaving your side until whoever is chasing us is surely gone," Jen told him, hands on her hips as she scolded.

"You don't have to worry about who was chasing us until tonight. Vampyre can't walk in the daylight. Go home and rest, do whatever and come back when it gets dark if you're still worried. Until then, I'm going to get some sleep myself."

Jax opened the hotel room door, but kept it closed enough that only he could walk through. Jen was either going to have to follow him, or his plan really was to shut her out before she could protest. Jax stepped into his room and quickly turned around to face her. She was right behind him.

"We can pick up the debate of what those men wanted later. I really need to sleep," Jax told her sternly. It was strange to be the older one when she felt so much like his sister. Actually, it was a little fun to be the older one bossing someone else around for a change.

"But it isn't safe," Jen whined. She had her full puppy dog eyes on him, like it was going to sway him to agree with him.

"You'll be fine. You were fine before I came here, and will be for a couple hours while I rest." Jen moved to walk forward, and Jax shut the door anyway.

"Jax," Jen called as she pounded on the door.

Jax didn't reply as he made his way to the bathroom to finally take a shower and then get some sleep. It didn't matter if she stood there all day pounding on the door. He had grown used to filtering out noises when he slept, and would still be able to feel if something was off. He didn't care if she stopped or not. And from the sounds of it, she wasn't going to give up without a fight. He should have kept her awake all night also, and then he wouldn't have had a problem. She'd have been too tired to fuss.

Not needing much rest after his shower, Jax got in a two-hour nap. At some point during his shower, she had given up trying to get his attention. Two hours of sleep left plenty of daylight hours to go exploring, once he had searched the Internet a bit more. He needed to know where his father was buried to see if there was a body there or not. He hoped there was a body, and that would mean that Wes Cunningham the vampyre was his brother. If there wasn't a body, Jax wasn't sure what to think.

After an hour's worth of reading page after page and calling a few places, Jax concluded that there were three cemeteries that Wes Cunningham could be buried in, because he wasn't in the other ones in town. Two were right in town, and the third was a ways out. He would have to drive to that one, so he decided it would be quickest to drive to all of them.

Once ready to leave, Jax grabbed his keys and opened his hotel room door. He wasn't prepared for the weight that dropped against him in the form of Jen, who had been leaning against it. She smiled up at him from her place sprawled on the floor.

"Going somewhere?" she asked with a bright smile as she sat up.

Jax stepped over her. He assumed when the knocking stopped that she had left. He'd even looked out the peephole to make sure, and hadn't seen her because she was seated and leaning against his door. Had he known that, he would have gone out the balcony to avoid seeing her now. He really didn't want to take her with him anywhere.

Turning around he motioned for her to move out of his doorway. Jen stood up, and Jax was able to close his door.

Then he moved around her and began to walk toward the staircase. Jen eagerly followed right behind him.

"Where we off to?" she asked.

Jax spun around quickly, and Jen bounced off his chest after running into him.

"*We* aren't going anywhere. I don't need some rich lawyer's niece following me around. You're going to go home, stay here, or whatever. I have stuff to do that doesn't include babysitting you. My offer to watch over you at night is it," Jax explained. Jen frowned at him.

Ignoring her, Jax turned back around and climbed down the stairs to the parking lot that held his bike. That was going to be an easy enough get away as he could just hop on and ride off. There would be nothing she could do about it.

Jax made his way out the side hallway of the hotel and to the garage with his bike. He was just about to turn the corner when he reached into his pocket for his keys. They were gone. Jax patted his other pockets to be sure he hadn't put them in a different one, but they were really gone. Searching his mind, Jax was certain he had brought his keys with. He had grabbed them right before walking out of his hotel room.

"Kind of hard to go anywhere without these," Jen said as she twirled his key chain around her finger.

"When did you…?" Jax began to ask, but he didn't need to finish. He had his keys when he left the room. He had his keys when he walked down the hallways and then she bumped into him. All pickpockets knew the whole bump into someone trick to take what they wanted.

"I may be a niece of a well-off lawyer, but that doesn't mean I don't know how to do a thing or two. My uncle gave me a roof over my head, but I got everything else I have myself."

"Without working, I guess," Jax added and held out his hand for his keys.

Jen plopped keys into Jax's hand and smiled sweetly at him. Jax wasn't sure what her plan was now, but when he looked at his hand, he understood. They weren't his keys, but the keys to the car she had borrowed from her uncle. After her quick snatch, he couldn't be sure she had asked for permission before borrowing the car.

"My keys, not yours." Jax held the keys back to her.

Jen began walking into the garage and to the waiting car. Jax had no choice but to follow her as he didn't have his keys yet. Jen stopped at the dark blue car they had been in the night before. She smiled at him as she waited to see what he would do.

"My keys," Jax repeated as he stared her down. He tried to use his serious face, but it was hard. It seemed like Jen was possibly just as stubborn as he was.

"Come on. Do you really want to go walking around cemeteries on your own?"

Jax looked at her and added a bit of a glare to his eyes. "Spying on me, too? Did you bug the room while I was getting dressed yesterday?"

Jen rolled her eyes. "I don't need to bug the room to figure out what you're up to. You want to know if your father is actually buried or not. That's why you're roaming around graveyards. I'm not an idiot. Anyone could guess that would be your next step. Well, anyone that knows you."

"And you know me?" Jax asked.

He moved quickly over to where she stood and knocked her against the car. It was enough to get her off balance to grab his keys out of her pocket before moving back to his original spot.

"I bet you thought I don't hit girls, and that I have all that honor crap people say about hunters." Jax smiled at Jen, dangling his motorcycle keys in the air. "Well, here's one more piece of information. Hunters care about human life, but I grew up with a sister. Girls are all the same if you ask me, and they just get in the way. Go home, Jen. I'll be back later."

Jax turned and walked away from her. She obviously

didn't take the hint as her shoes padded along behind him while he walked. Jax really didn't care if she followed because there wasn't room on his bike for her to join him. He was going to just leave her. It wasn't like she wasn't safe in the hotel for the day, or probably her own house. Her uncle would know enough not to invite vampyres into his home. It was probably the only safe place he had.

Making it to his bike, Jax's quick getaway was dashed. Someone had taken a bike lock and put it on the front wheel of his motorcycle. Jax turned to Jen. She smiled at him sweetly for the second time. That was why she was following without a complaint. She hadn't just been sitting at his room for hours while he slept.

"You know I can just cut that off," Jax told her.

Now Jen pouted at him. It would be easy enough to remove.

"Why can't you just take me with? Consider it training. Maybe we'll run into a night human, and you can show me how you take them down in real life. Come on, let me go with."

Jax shook his head. It was against his better judgment to let her go with him. She was obviously tricky, and he wasn't sure what her plan was, or why she was determined to stick around him. He suspected that she was working for the vampyre to keep tabs on him, but she did seem genuinely afraid when she knew who they were. They might have been threatening her physically, or even pressuring her family to work with them. Jax still felt like the facts didn't add up, and that she was hiding something. Maybe a drive around town would get her to talk more and give him a clue as to what it was. Okay. He could play her game a little bit, but he was going to get answers.

They were already on the way to the third cemetery by

mid-afternoon. The first two in town didn't lead to anything. It hadn't been quick, but they had found their answer. Rows and rows of tombs with no Cunningham's buried there. Jax wasn't going to let it bother him. He was on a mission to get two goals taken care of at one time. If Wes wasn't at the last cemetery, then he would have to come up with another plan, but for now he was going to use positive thinking.

It was easy to get Jen to talk. She liked to talk … a lot. She told him about her life. She hated school and skipped a lot to run around town instead. She was raised by her uncle and aunt after her parents died, and they didn't seem to care what she did.

She was determined to find out why her parents had died. That was the main reason she needed to be trained by Jax, or so she said. Like many people around town, her parents' obituary said that they died in a car crash, but she remembered their car was home the night they had died. She had seen it herself, and though she was only five at the time, she was certain they left on a walk and just never came home.

Jax found her stories of life in New Orleans amusing, but he could tell she was still hiding something. It had been ten years since her parents died and he was sure she knew more. She wasn't telling, though, so that didn't help. He was going to have to play friendly a bit longer, but he was sure he was close to getting the truth. She obviously trusted him enough to be driving out in the middle of nowhere to go to a cemetery.

Pulling off the main road, Jax headed to the isolated cemetery that was the last one to check for the day. He had hoped this one wouldn't be where they needed to look, but he had a feeling it would be. The older graveyard was more worn, and it wasn't going to be fun to read all the gravestones in it, searching for just one name. It was going to take time, and he had to be out long before sunset. He still needed to make a plan how to keep away from whoever was looking for them. He doubted it was a one night deal.

Jax pulled the car to the only building there. He climbed out, and Jen followed, still chatting away about how she skipped the whole last week of classes and no one cared. Her school didn't even notice, let alone her aunt and uncle.

Together, they walked through the gate to the building. It was a structure of sorts, but had open doorways that kept the place the same temperature as the air outside. Jax led the way across the stone floor and looked around. There were two hallways jutting off the main entrance, and they were possibly ten feet long themselves. On either side of the hallways were tombs from the floor to the ceiling. Jax took it as a good sign as it seemed that the vampyre liked to pretend to be dead in mausoleums.

"You do know this is getting creepier and creepier, right? At least the last place was clean. This place needs a good scrub, like yesterday," Jen complained.

"I'm sure if you want to bring your mop and bucket, they wouldn't stop you," Jax responded as he walked toward the left hallway and began reading the names on the tombs.

It didn't take long to find the one labeled Wesley Cunningham. It was one of the cleaner ones in the place, as if it had recently been opened or used for that matter. Jax looked around. The place was empty, and more so the whole cemetery seemed to be empty. If he wanted to snoop, now was the perfect time.

"Keep a lookout," Jax said to Jen, who was standing on the other side reading names.

"You found it?" she asked in disbelief. After searching through two whole cemeteries, she seemed to doubt they were ever going to find it.

"Yes, and now I just need to look inside," Jax told her, taking out a knife and prying the face off the tomb.

Jax got part of the façade off the tomb. The marble surface was placed perfectly on the front, but Jax could tell that it wasn't going anywhere. Someone had permanently sealed the tomb. He wasn't going to get to the steel inside door to open and look inside. He'd already assumed that much, but hoped he could try. Not having answers stunk. And the one to give him answers was far from being trustworthy. Jax wasn't about to go talk to Wes Cunningham himself. Enough dealing with night humans over the years made Jax understand they couldn't be trusted.

"So this is a no-go?" Jen asked as Jax stood back up and put his pocket knife away.

"Seems so, unless you have any suggestions?"

"Um, hunters don't come with superhuman strength?" Jen teased.

Jax shook his head. Yes, he was stronger than an average person, but not strong enough to pull stone from a wall it was fixed to without some sort of power tool.

"Guess it's back to the hotel to do some more digging," Jax said as they came out of the tombs and back to their waiting car. Jax casually glanced around the cemetery. They were still alone, but he had a feeling that they weren't really alone. It was like a sixth sense was going off. Jax peeked into the car before opening the door, and decided to double check the trunk just in case.

"Something wrong?" Jen asked as Jax popped the trunk and looked inside at the empty space.

It was weird. It felt like someone was there, but then it felt like they weren't. He couldn't quite grasp what he was feeling. Shaking his head to help clear it, Jax walked back to the driver's seat. It all just felt funny, but there was nothing he could do about that, or even explain it to Jen. Something was just off.

Pulling out of the cemetery, Jax glanced back one more time. He didn't know why it felt strange, but what could he do? Jax turned right to head back to town and began picking up speed on the open road. Jen was talking about something new, but he wasn't paying attention because he couldn't shake the feeling that something was wrong. As they crested the top of a small hill and started down the other side as they picked up speed, Jax slammed on the brakes to try to stop from hitting a car at the base of the hill that was passing someone else. Jax hated dumb drivers, but luckily they were far enough away. At least he thought they were far enough away … until he realized his car wasn't slowing down. Jax pressed the brake all the way to the floor, and nothing happened. Actually, he felt the car accelerate because he was driving downhill now; perfect timing for the brakes to fail. Jax knew enough about cars to know it wasn't likely that his brakes just stopped working. There was something up, and it looked like Jax wasn't going to get the chance to figure it out. His body was flung into the steering wheel, and bones crunched as he felt the life drain from him.

CHAPTER 7

Sucking in his breath, Jax opened his eyes. He expected to feel pain beyond belief as he was sure he'd broken most of the bones in his body. Healing from it would be excruciatingly painful. He thought he'd even felt his neck snap. That would be a pain to heal from. But it wasn't the case. Jax was driving out of the cemetery again. He kept his foot off the gas and let the car just coast, knowing the brakes were gone.

"Something wrong?" Jen asked Jax for a second time.

Then it sunk in. Jax had died just moment ago when he ran into the other car. It was his new sense taking over to keep him safe. Jax hadn't yet gotten used to the weird feeling of dying and coming back. He had hoped that by leaving the hunters that it would go away also, but it didn't seem to be the case. Jax was still predicting the future, but at least it was keeping him alive.

"Do you have your phone with you?" Jax asked. His was back in the hotel, forgotten, because of how they had left. It wasn't like he turned it on when he was out investigating, but it wasn't like him to forget to bring it with at all.

"Yeah, but it's dead," Jen said, holding up the phone.

Jax wasn't about to go to the right again and instead turned left. Time to get a different ending to their situation.

"Um, the map says we need to go back the other way." Jen held up the paper map they had used to get to the grave that held no answers.

"Not today," Jax replied as he completed the turn.

The road was flat, and he was half tempted to just drive into a ditch to get the car to stop. And had he been anywhere with less rain, he would have. Now he wasn't as sure with the ditches filled with water, mud, and whatever creatures lived there. He had already experienced death by car accident today; he didn't want to try death by being drowned or maybe eaten. And he wasn't sure his sense would allow him to come back twice. So far, he had made the right choice the second time and continued living.

Jax took the road as slowly as he could and didn't use the gas at all. Unfortunately, they were coasting well. Without being able to slow down, the first serious corner was going to be a problem. Jax went at a slow enough speed to make Jen stare at him.

"What's going on now? Did you turn into a grandma because you've been in cemeteries all day?" she finally asked after Jax refused to offer an explanation.

"We have no brakes," Jax replied as he continued to analyze the road in front of him.

The road had a slight decline that was making the car pick up speed. Jax was still weighing his options of what to do. It looked like farther ahead there was less water and the hill was going to head back up … at least he hoped it was heading up.

"Look at the map to see what the best way to get back to the highway would be," Jax told Jen. After he crashed the car they were going to have to walk. He figured that would give her something to do other than just ask questions.

The drive they were taking was safe. No hill or sharp corners, and a farm field to the left of the road. Jax kept his eyes on the field. It would be a perfect crash point if there was a way into the field that didn't include the watery ditch. Jax kept driving at his slow pace, searching for a ramp from the road onto the field.

"Um, problem," Jen said as she peered down at the map.

"Problem?" Jax was still looking for a way onto the farm field.

"Yes. This road is ending at a T. You're going to have to turn soon and into possible traffic."

Jax grabbed the map from her. She reached over him and pointed to a space on the map. Jax glanced down at it quickly before looking back to the pasture. They had just passed it, and now there was dense brush on both sides of the road. Jax looked again at the map. It was more than a problem. There was no way he was going to make a sharp right or left turn going the speed he was.

"What do we do?" Jen asked.

"Put your belt on and prepare for impact," Jax replied and tried to give her a smile. It was a strained, but still a smile. He wasn't afraid of a crash. He had lived through worse, but he didn't like not knowing about other cars. That was what killed him the last time.

Jen did exactly what Jax told her to do. If only she was as good at listening at other times. She looked terrified, and Jax could see the road ending in the distance. They were still surrounded by trees, but at least the water was gone. *Good. No lurking reptiles that would eat him for lunch.* He just needed to crash the car the safest way possible now since there was a slight gradient downhill. The car wasn't going to stop on its own any time soon.

"I'm going to try to spin the car around to make the back end take the brunt of the hit. No matter what I do, we'll need to hit something to stop. Right now, our best bet is to hit the trees here without taking the chance of pulling into unknown traffic. I promise you this is going to not be fun, but it's better than running into traffic."

Stretching his neck, Jax felt a crack. Yes, he didn't want to try breaking his neck again. Jax was pretty sure Jen had never purposely crashed a car before. Well, he hadn't either, but he had done a lot of stupid things to get hurt over the years, like talking back to his mother.

The intersection was coming closer. He needed to do it soon. Jen double checked her seatbelt and nodded to him. She understood that they had to do something. She hadn't had the privilege of remembering they died the first time, so she didn't look as terrified as Jax felt internally. At least they weren't coming down a large hill. The speed was just constant for the time being.

Taking a deep breath, Jax pulled the car off the road, jerking the wheel back to try to keep the back end on the gravel. Hitting something caused the car to spin, and Jax let go of the wheel to brace his face as the car slammed against the trees, forcing the front end of the car to whip forward and crash into a different patch of trees.

The car jolted to a stop and metal crunched as they hit thicker trees than the first ones, which had given way when they snapped. Jax held on as he was jostled around by the car and smacked into the large white airbags, but he felt no breaking or snapping of bones in his body. It was definitely an upgrade from the previous try. The car sputtered a little, and Jax sniffed the air for smoke as the bags deflated. Crashing a car was one thing, but he didn't want to blow it up.

Jen moaned from the seat beside him. The bags left a large mass of white fabric on their laps, but neither one of them seemed to be seriously hurt.

"Let's get out of here and then we can rest before we walk to get help," Jax said.

There was no way he was going to wait around to meet whoever did this. He had a gut feeling that it was foul play, and his gut was rarely wrong. They could have easily been waiting to follow and take them from the accident if they weren't dead.

"Yeah," Jen said. "While that was fun, I think I want to stay in the hotel next time."

Jax smiled at her. He was pretty sure crashing a car was the most dangerous thing she had ever done. Jax pushed on his door and found it was stuck. Pulling off his seatbelt, he turned to kick the door. There was a dent on the outside that stopped it from easily being pushed open, but it moved just fine with a kick. Jax stepped out of the car and stretched to see how bad it was. Scratches lined the car from back to front along with a few large dents. He had a feeling Jen's uncle was never going to lend her a car again.

Jax looked back in the car. Jen was still in her seat.

"Is your door stuck?" Jax asked. He walked around the car to the other side. Her door was pushed against a tree. "Come out my door," he suggested.

Jen pushed the deflated airbag off of her lap and moved to climb over the center console to his seat before stopping.

"What's wrong?" Jax asked as he poked his head into the car. She looked up at him, and he could immediately tell something wasn't right.

Jax jumped back in the car and started to pull her airbag away. Her seatbelt was off, but she didn't leave her seat. Jax whipped out his pocketknife and cut the white fabric before tossing it in the crunched-up backseat.

"What's wrong?" he asked again as he got rid of the last of the airbag.

"The seat moved when we hit one of the trees. I didn't notice, I'm stuck," Jen explained as Jax could finally see her legs completely. Her right foot was pushed between the seat and door with a piece of metal going through the bracelet she wore on her leg. She didn't seem to be bleeding, though.

"Can you move it at all?" Jax leaned across her lap and tried to move her foot.

"Ouch," she scolded him as he pulled on her foot. The bracelet kept her foot in place.

"Is your foot hurt?"

"I think something's broken, but it's not bleeding," Jen replied as she stared down at it, confirming what he suspected

"Then it's going to hurt a lot when I pull it out, but we can't sit around here. Someone cut the brakes. We need to get moving before they come looking for us."

Jen appeared shocked at his words. She hadn't thought it was foul play. Now she seemed worried.

"If I cut your bracelet off, I should be able to—"

"No," Jen yelled at him and pushed him back, narrowly missing being cut by his open blade. "I can't take my bracelet off."

Jax sat back in his crushed seat and stared at her.

"You have two options," he said calmly. "Either we take the bracelet off and get out of here, or you wait here with it on until I can make it back to get help. By the time I walk back to town and get help, it will be dark. Do you really want to be sitting around here in a beat-up car when it gets dark?"

Jen chewed on her lip. She seriously didn't want the bracelet to come off, and Jax wasn't sure how much more he would need to say to scare her into letting him help her. It was just a strand of metal with beads on it. How in the world was she even trying to decide? Bracelets were replaceable; lives were not.

"I know if it were up me to, I'd let the family heirloom be broken and get to live rather than try to protect it and die in the process," Jax told her. He couldn't be certain anything would happen to her, but since danger seemed to follow him—and her, too—he thought the chances were high.

"If you cut it off, everything will change. You won't help me anymore."

"Help you? I'm pretty sure you're the one that locked up my bike to force me to take you along."

"I can't explain it without showing you, but I promise you, this will change everything. Promise me that you will still help me train. Promise me," Jen begged. Something was really up with her.

Jax didn't need to hesitate. A bracelet breaking wouldn't change anything.

"Promise me," she repeated.

"That I'll still train you?"

Jen nodded.

"I can't train you if you're dead, so let me cut it off, and the answer is still yes."

Jen let out the breath she was holding. Jax didn't hesitate to reach down, ready to cut off the jewelry.

"Stop," she told him.

Jax huffed. Girls were so finicky, changing their minds all the time.

"It can't be cut off. It needs my blood to come off," she told him.

Now Jax was interested in the bracelet. When it was just a metal chain, he didn't understand. But something that needed blood to be removed meant it was enchanted. He had met more than a few witches and night humans that could cast spells. Maybe he was too rash in his choice to save her after all. Jax looked at her where she sat. She was as afraid of the bracelet coming off as meeting the night humans chasing them. He wasn't sure what it meant, but he had promised her. He was going to find out because he couldn't leave her behind.

"I hit my head. You can use that blood," she suggested, flattening herself to the seat to allow Jax to sit up a little and wipe the blood from her face. "You have to touch my blood to the white bead, and it will snap off."

Jax took the blood on his finger and bent back down to look at the various beads on the bracelet.

"Just remember that you promised me," Jen said one more time.

"Nothing changes as long as you don't turn into a blood-hungry monster that wants to kill me."

Jen gave a little laugh as Jax found the white bead. When he smeared the fresh blood on it, the chain snapped open just as easily as she said it would. Jax stayed by her foot and wiggled it a bit. She would be able to pull it out now, but she was right—it looked like she had a broken foot. It was going to make the walk back long, but it was better than sitting in the car.

"See, not a problem. You can get out now," Jax told her

as he pulled back to his seat and looked up to offer her his hand.

Jen sat in the seat perfectly still, staring at him. Her auburn curls were straight, and her blue eyes looked almost eerily white. Her flushed skin had paled, and she stared back at him. Jax was at a loss for words. He could feel it. Without a doubt, Jen was a vampyre.

Jax jumped out of the car, and Jen wiggled a little to free her foot before following him. The pain didn't seem to register with her about her newly broken foot. She was too busy staring at Jax. She scooted over to the edge of the driver's seat and just sat, staring at him.

"You promised," Jen said. Even her voice was different, smoother sounding.

"I promised as long as you didn't turn into a bloodsucker that wants to kill me," Jax replied.

"And I don't want to kill you," she added.

Jax kept his distance. He didn't need to touch her to know what she was. He knew, but it made no sense whatsoever. He had shaken her hand before. There hadn't been a trace of night human in her then. Now, without the bracelet, she was one. Even stranger was seeing her sitting in the sunlight. Vampyres couldn't be in direct sunlight, yet there she was.

"I don't understand. What are you?"

"I'm pretty sure you already figured that out. They say hunters have a sixth sense about night humans." Jen sat perfectly still as she watched him. Her foot was already bruising under the swelling, but no doubt it was trying to heal.

"I get that part of it. How? Why are you one now?" Jax asked.

"All I know is my father is a vampyre, and my mother is human. From everything I ever found on them, vampyre can only turn people into other vampyres. They can't have a child. I figure maybe because my mother was a priestess of her coven that could be why I was born, but no one has answers for me. I was hoping the hunters would know more, but I get the feeling I'm the only half night human you've met, or you would have figured it out sooner." Jen shrugged, but didn't move out of the car.

"Why do you fear the vampyre then?" Jax asked, his head swirling with questions. This was just the first one that popped out. She chose to show her secret over being left for the vampyre to find.

"Because they don't know about me. The bracelet keeps my vampyre side hidden, but if I get too upset or close to death, she comes out. I don't want them to know what I am. I get more answers around town when they think I'm a normal person. If they find out about me and being able to walk in sunlight, they won't let me go, ever."

"So the whole 'my parents are dead' thing … is that even true?"

"My mother is dead. She used her life to create the bracelet to let me live a normal life. She never told anyone who my father is, and yes, I've been raised by my uncle. And no, he doesn't know about this."

Jax nodded. This made things more complicated. As Jax stared at Jen, he could still see the teen that was driving him nuts behind this new version of her, but he wasn't sure he could trust her now. She was a bloodsucker, and even if she didn't want to kill him, she was still one of them.

"So are you going to stake me now or later?" she asked.

"Stake you?"

"Isn't that what hunters do? They kill night humans. I happen to be half night human."

Jax ran his hand through his hair. "I don't just run around killing night humans. I kill those that break the law, but I don't randomly kill them unless they attack first. Anyone attacking me is fair game."

"I don't plan to attack you, and your blood smells weird anyway."

This wasn't the first time he had been told that, but he didn't have time to ask more. They needed to get going and figure the rest out later.

"Then we should be fine. We do need to get out of here though," Jax said as he glanced up at the sky again. It was still light out and would be for a few more hours, but he had a feeling it would take at least that long to get back to town.

"Go ahead and leave me," Jen suggested. "My foot is far more broken than I could tell before. There are at least five fractures. I can feel them trying to grow back together, but like all night humans, my recovery is based on blood. I haven't been in this form in over a year, so there isn't much for my body to use to heal."

"After you just told me that you want to keep this form a secret, you plan to stay here?" Jax shook his head. Girls really were confusing.

"Not much I can do. My foot is broken and will be for at least a few more hours. I might heal enough to get out of here, but you should leave now. Once I'm healed, I can run faster than you can. Don't worry about me." Jen gave Jax a smile, but he wasn't buying it. It wasn't genuine.

"Fine," Jax muttered as he walked closer while flipping out his knife.

Jen appeared alarmed.

Jax sliced through the palm of his hand. "Feed quickly. I heal probably almost as fast as you do."

Jen stared at him for a moment.

"I won't be offering a second time," Jax added as she grabbed his hand.

Jax had never fed a night human before and found it strange. He only had a few friends that were night humans because they were the good kind. From what Jax had read and could remember of vampyres, they weren't especially good, but for some reason, Jax still saw the night human in front of him as Jen. She was still herself. It didn't make complete sense, but he didn't think there was any bad in her.

"I don't want to be this way," Jen said as she pulled back, wiping the blood from her lips. "I want to find out how to stay human all the time. I believe my mother thought that the bracelet wouldn't ever come off, but I have to take it off at least once a year. The night human side of me just doesn't go away. I wish it would. I'd do anything to stay human all the time."

Stepping back, Jax gazed at her. He offered her the bracelet, and Jen smiled as she took it.

"It might be easier to wait until we're closer to town to put it back on," Jax suggested. "I'm guessing this form of yours can keep up with me better."

Jen smirked at the thought. She might say she wanted to be a normal human all the time, but it seemed like her vampyre side might like to stick around, too. Perhaps it was the first time that Jen saw her vampyre side as an advantage.

"Can you wait like five minutes?"

Jax was about to ask why when she disappeared from sight. He could feel a night human presence running away from him; it had to be her. Going back to the car, he retrieved all his stuff from the trunk. He never went anywhere without extra weapons. Jax had his bag around his shoulder when Jen appeared in front of him again. She hadn't been gone five minutes.

"So, I found those at the cemetery," she explained, pointing to two bicycles laying on the road. "I know it's not your type of bike, but I figure this way I can go back to being me. And I also went into the tomb—super night human strength you know. There wasn't a body there. And lastly, I looked around the place. I could smell the leftovers of night humans there, too. Maybe the brake issue was night humans, but they were long gone by the time I was there. They'd have to be working with a regular human because they can't be in the sunlight." Jen tapped her finger on her lip. "Yep. I think that's everything."

Reaching down, Jen pricked the tip of her finger to touch her blood to the bead as she clasped the bracelet back around her newly healed ankle. Instantly, she was back to her former self.

"See? Still me," Jen said as she twirled around in a circle.

Jax nodded. She was back to being day human Jen and the night human in her was completely hidden, but it was still there. The night human side knew it was there, too. Jen was another mystery added to his already growing list.

"Ready for a nice, long ride back to town?" Jax asked. He was trying not to do a double take and study her further. He had never met anyone in his life that could be both a day and night human. He didn't know it was possible. He thought it was one drop of blood that made you a night human, but he was certain she was only a day human now. It was strange.

"Maybe I should have stayed in my vampyre form," Jen complained as Jax walked over to the bicycles and handed one over to her.

"I'll be as nice to you as I was yesterday while working out. In fact, we can consider this our workout for today." Jax smiled at her, and she groaned.

Jax hadn't been on a bicycle in years, but it didn't matter. Kind of like fighting night humans; once you knew how, it was easy to just pick up and do it again. But it was hard to look at Jen now and not see her night human side. He had so many questions, and she probably couldn't answer most of them. The ride back was only going to give him more time to come up with questions that no one could answer. Not to mention her news that no one was in his father's tomb, which made things even more complicated. However, for the time being, it was best to get back to the safety of his hotel room. Then he could ponder it all.

CHAPTER 8

Jax was able to convince Jen to go back to her uncle's place for the night, as he needed some rest and time to think about everything. He ran off to New Orleans for answers and hadn't been able to find any yet. There were just more questions. Now, throwing the Jen confusion into the mix was amplifying how much he didn't know. Jax needed time alone.

In all his years in classes and talking with hunters from all over the country, Jax had never heard of someone being born part night human. The way it typically worked was all or nothing. If you had a gene to be a night human, you became one, and if you didn't, then you didn't. There was never an in-between, though technically Jen wasn't in between. Without her bracelet, she was all night human. Maybe that was it. Her mother had spelled her to stay human so that she wouldn't become a night human. That was an explanation, but with Jen's mother dead, Jax couldn't find out if his guess was correct.

After tossing and turning as long as he could, Jax decided it was shower time instead. It was all too confusing to think about. If it was possible to be half night human, what did that mean? He had never met anyone like Jen before. He had to wonder if it was a witch thing. Maybe that was the key to her, but there would be no way of knowing.

Jax finished his shower and came into his room in just his towel. Then he froze in place. Sitting on his balcony was the one person he wasn't expecting: Wes Cunningham.

"I hear you've been asking around for this." Wes held up a yellow folder— the exact yellow folder that started this whole mess.

"I've been asking for answers," Jax replied.

"Well, I'm here and will answer all that I can," Wes replied, staying in his seat.

Jax was thankful that vampyre couldn't enter a residence without explicit permission. As the room was rented to Jax, his night human father would have to remain where he was. Jax was at least safe from the strongest night human he had ever met. Just because the man was potentially his father meant nothing to him; Jax was still a hunter, and this man was still a night human. Since his arrival in New Orleans only days ago, Jax had killed two of the vampyre himself. Jax wasn't sure if his father knew or not, but it was safe to say that being separated in two different rooms was a positive thing for Jax.

"So will you confirm that you're a night human?" Jax asked, although he already knew the answer.

"Yes."

"And you knew who I was when we met the other day?"

"Yes. You caught me off guard. I wasn't expecting my own son to show up to the business party that I was throwing. It has been years since I've seen you, so I should have known it was you, but really … you've changed a lot since you were a teen."

Jax sucked in his breath. This was his father. He hadn't asked yet, but he'd had a feeling that it was true anyway when there was no body in the tomb. The man sitting before him was the father his mother never mentioned, and Jax knew why now. If the man chose to turn into a vampyre rather than raise his kids; well, that would be reason enough for his mother to hate him for the rest of her life.

"I'm really yours?" Jax had to ask to be absolutely sure.

Sitting down on the bed, he stared at the man. He didn't need an answer. It was true. He could see it in the man's face and the nose they shared. There was really no denying it, but Jax wanted another verbal confirmation. Maybe there was a small part of him that wanted it to not be true, that wanted his father to be just a regular old person who Jax could leave the night human world to be with, someone not related to the mess Jax lived daily.

"Yes, Jax. You are my son, and Jade is my daughter. While I wanted to be a father to you, you can understand that your mother and I might not see eye-to-eye."

That would be putting it mildly. While Jax didn't hunt night humans for sport and only went on assigned missions, there were more than a few hunters that just liked to kill them. They felt that no matter what, night humans were dangerous, and if they could find some sort of small clause in a mission to keep hunting, they would. His mother was one of those. She was on a mission to rid the world of the bloodsuckers. Yes, Jax understood why his father was never invited to family holidays.

"So are you going to explain to me why you chose to be a leech rather than raise your kids?" Okay, that was a little disrespectful, but Jax was a bit upset to know the truth of his father.

"We'll have to save my night human origins for another time," Wes replied.

"And this folder?" Jax patted the spot on the bed next to him where it landed when his father tossed it in the room.

"That explains everything I have willed to you. What bank accounts you can access when you turn eighteen and a little family history. It should be able to tell you more about the vampyre clan than what the hunters probably taught you."

Jax held in the laugh he was going to have at that one later. Vampyres were one of the few clans they really didn't learn about at all. According to the hunter books, vampyres were basically extinct. Then again, Jax had spent the last part of the school year with a new night human friend that was also an extinct species, and her clan was alive and thriving. Jax was beginning to see that perhaps the hunters had a very limited view of the world.

"So, I'm going to guess your mother doesn't know you're here," Wes commented as Jax didn't reply.

"No. I decided my graduation present to myself was to take a road trip and find out where this mysterious check was came from. If I asked her, she wouldn't answer," Jax explained a little about what had led him on his trip.

He wanted the night human across from him to know he wasn't there on a mission. He wanted his father to know that Jax was just there for answers. While Wes seemed to just walk away the day before, he was there now. Jax was getting more out of the man right now than his mother had told him his whole life, and they had only spoken for a few minutes.

"She probably would've sent you off on a mission if she knew. Rommy can be a little protective of you two," Wes chuckled. He seemed to know Jax's mother well.

Jax's eyes bugged at the laughing night human. "Protective? It was only a month ago she broke my wrist because I was going to interfere with Jade's hunter test. Protective doesn't describe how she feels about Jade and me."

Wes gave Jax a smile. "I could tell you stories that would change your mind on that. While she's a little rough, she'd never do anything to actually harm you."

Jax shook his head. His and Wes's view of harm seemed to differ. Then again, the man sitting outside his room wasn't a regular human. Maybe to him, his mother's treatment was fair.

"So how is the famed night human hunter Rommy doing?" Wes asked casually, but Jax could sense more behind it.

"Probably off killing something as we speak. She hasn't checked in with me yet, but why would she care? I'm just a son." Wes had to have been with his mother long enough to see that the men in the hunter world were treated differently. Maybe that was why he became a night human. Maybe Wes didn't like being a second-class citizen either.

"Would you like me to call her and inform her that you've come to visit me?" Wes smiled. This time it looked devious.

"Yeah, *no thanks* on that one. She's probably already mad enough at me. I don't need extra broken bones because you called her. Any time we asked as kids about you, it would anger her enough that we stopped. I have a feeling she knows what you are and that doesn't sit well with her."

Wes laughed. "Your mother knows I'm a vampyre. And yes, *doesn't sit well* is one way to describe it."

Jax didn't find that as funny as the man across from him did. It was strange to look at the vampyre. He looked like he could be his older brother, not his father. The age thing was odd enough, but there was something more to the man. It was the power emanating off him. It was like he was the most powerful night human Jax had ever met. Which really wasn't saying much, since his new ability to sense night humans was growing each day. Maybe there were others like Wes, but now Jax felt it ever more strongly. His gut was telling him that Wes Cunningham was different.

"Have you been keeping track of us all these years?" Part of Jax wanted to ask if his father knew where to send money, and why didn't he come and take him away from the hunters instead of running off and turning himself into a night human monster. But he had a feeling that question wouldn't be answered.

"I found you when you were four. Until then, your mother had hidden you and your sister well. She ran from me when you were only days old. I honestly thought I'd never see you again. Since I've found you, there's always been someone there watching over you and reporting back to me. I'd do it myself, but we're in complete agreement that your mother would probably try to stake me if I came anywhere near you or Jade."

Jax tried to process all of what Wes had just said. First off was the whole running away thing. Why the heck did his mother run from his father? Why didn't she stay with him and keep him from turning into a night human? Second was Jax had caught that Wes said his mother would try to stake him. The key word was *try*. Wes was suggesting Jax's "all-wonderful night human hunting mother" wouldn't be able to kill him. Maybe his judgment of the older man's power was correct.

"Staking people who come to visit seems to be the way people greet you here in New Orleans. I think I can officially say that there have been three attempts on my life, and I've been here less than a week."

"Wait, what attempts?" Wes's happy, playful mood was gone in an instant. The power from the man flared a little. Jax was pretty sure without even knowing him well that the man was getting mad.

"Don't worry. I'm not that easy to kill. I've been doing this long enough that I could see it coming. When I went to the office of Lawrence and Sons, they tried to keep me there. It might have been just until you arrived, but I high-tailed it out of there before finding out. Then there were the guys that followed me out of your party. And today someone cut my brakes when I was looking for your tomb. I get the feeling that there are some people that don't want you and me talking."

"Cut your brakes?" Wes was getting angrier by the second. Jax didn't think there could be more power in the man, but he was more than certain now that what he felt was only a fraction of his strength.

"Yeah, lucky for me I have this whole new 'save yourself' sense that kicks in. It seems like fate wants me to live, so I get a do over. I was able to crash the car and walk away from it. The car probably isn't going to go anywhere, but what can you do?" Jax wasn't too worried about it. Jen said she would take care of it, and he was going to let her. After all, she was the one with a rich uncle.

"Okay. We'll talk about fate and you later. For now, I

need to go check on a few things. You'll be safe from now on."

Wes rose from his seat and then disappeared. Jax could see that he jumped, but he had no clue if it was up or down because the man moved so fast. Just like that, his first private meeting with his father was over, and he finally got one answer. Wes Cunningham *was* his father, and even though he was a night human, he was still living. Jax wanted to call his sister and tell her about it, but he was pretty sure his mother would show up under the time it took Jade to get there, and Rommy would create enough of a scene that Jax would never get more answers. For now, he was going to go with what he had and leave the folder alone. Wes hadn't answered the one question he needed to know to trust the man. Why did he decide to turn into a monster?

Jax was happy to get out of the cramped hotel gym area, and back to his own room to shower and clean up after his second workout with Jen. She seemed to be a fast learner, and Jax enjoyed teaching her how to defend herself. Part of him thought of canceling now that he knew she was part night human, as everything he taught her could be used against a hunter, but he was pretty certain she only wanted to defend herself. And after his brief stay in New Orleans, he didn't blame her. It seemed like every other day someone was attacking them—and it was likely him that they were attacking since everyone knew he was a hunter. He was hoping it was their day off.

Jen had left already, and Jax was going to take the evening off to debate with himself for a second night whether or not he wanted to read the folder his father had left. Jax shook his head. Wes Cunningham might have contributed DNA, but he wasn't a father. Jax wasn't sure what he was going to call the guy. He had spent his whole childhood wishing the man would turn up, and now that he found him it was a bit of a disappointment to find that he wasn't human.

"I see you didn't have time to do some reading," Wes said from the balcony.

"I wasn't sure if I wanted to or not."

Jax had remembered to bring clothing into the bathroom this time, so he didn't have to sit in a towel when his father showed up unannounced. He was not going to take a shower without bringing clothing with him the rest of his trip. Meeting your long-lost father was awkward enough, but to think afterwards that you did it in a towel was beyond embarrassing.

"I'm sorry I had to take off last night like that. It seems there's a breakdown in communication within the vampyre world right now. I think I have it fixed, but please do tell me if you run into any more problems."

Jax nodded his head. How was he supposed to tell the man he didn't know anything about, let alone his phone number, if something happened?

"Problems seem to follow me and this mark," Jax stated, pointing to his arm.

"Yes, another unfortunate decision of your mother's."

"So you and my mom ..." Jax really wanted to know as much as he could.

"We were matched up," Wes replied. "No one could handle your mother, but it seemed the hunters felt I could."

"Matched up? Like an arranged marriage?"

Smiling, Wes nodded. "Sure. That would be a good description of it."

"And she went along with that? I can't imagine my mother agreeing to having anything arranged for her." There seemed to be more that Jax didn't know, but that was life with his mother. She rarely told him or Jade anything.

"Surprisingly, she did. I think at some point she might have loved me, but if I went anywhere close to you or Jade since she left, she would have killed me in a heartbeat. She never loved me as much as she loved you two."

That was much more than he expected of his parents. Then again, his mother refused to talk about Wes, and so Jax and Jade had to make up all what they thought they were missing. They wanted to believe their father was dead or lost on an abandoned island, and that was why he never came for them. They weren't the only ones. Lots of the hunters had kids without fathers, but there were ones with loving, doting dads. Jade and Jax wished for that more times than they could count.

"So why'd she run off? Did you become a night human and scare her off?"

Wes smiled.

"Why don't you read the file? That would answer some questions, or at least make you realize that there's much you don't know. Your mother has done an excellent job of keeping both you and Jade in the dark. I figured by now she would have told you guys more, what with Jade joining the hunters as a full hunter, but again, Rommy surprises me. She's left out major details. I don't know why she doesn't see it as important. I mean, she felt it was important enough to change your name, but that took her over ten years."

"Change my name?" Jax had been called Jax as long as he remembered. "What was my name on my birth certificate?"

"You wouldn't believe me if I told you," Wes replied and laughed. Jax didn't see what was funny. His mother had changed his name without him knowing it. For that matter, though, Jax had never seen his birth certificate. "It should be one of the top papers in the file."

Jax stared at the man that was his father. Was he trying to get him to open the folder? What was the point? Jax had the man in front of him. He could just tell him.

"Seriously. You have to see what it was and then I'll explain it to you," Wes replied.

Jax wanted to tell him no—he could feel his mother's defiance flare up in him—but he also could see the eyes of the man that was his father. Jax had seen night humans over the years, hundreds of them. While he didn't like that they fed on humans like they were food—because technically they were food to them—he did know that some of them weren't bad. Many wouldn't hesitate to kill a person, but others protected them. Jax had the misfortune of dealing more with the ones that didn't care about humans, but he had met a few who were truly good people. As he stared at his father, he got the sense that there wasn't any inherent evil in the man. That didn't mean he hadn't done bad things, but the man wasn't evil.

Reaching next to him, Jax flipped open the file. There on top was a birth certificate for Sage Kristian. Jax scratched his head. He didn't have a sister named Sage, so it made no sense whatsoever. Jax looked more at it and was stumped why this girl had the same birthday as him, and was born to Rommy and Wes. That really made no sense. Jax looked up to Wes.

"I told you you wouldn't believe me if I said your mother registered you as Sage, my second daughter," Wes replied. "Luckily for you, she did finally go correct that a few years ago. Probably around the time you were getting your driver's license and would ask questions."

"Not possible. I think I'd have remembered if I was a girl, and I'm sure that my parts are originals." Jax just stared at the document.

"Oh, I know you're a boy, and so did your mother. That's why she lied about it," Wes answered. "The agreement I had with your mother was that any daughter born was hers to raise, and any son was mine. She agreed with me, but once she had you, she decided not to honor that agreement. I was a bit too trusting of your mother to check your gender. When she registered you as a girl, I assumed that was the case. Then she took off and left me. I expected her to leave, but not so suddenly and without a good-bye. It wasn't until I found you guys almost four years later that I realized I had been lied to, and by then you were protected. There was no way I could get you back. You are the son I've been waiting for, and I wish I could have been there to raise you instead of leaving you with the hunters."

Jax stared at him. That wasn't what he was expecting in the least. His mother had secrets, but that was one that topped the cake in Jax's mind. He was going to need time to think it all over. There were more papers in the file, and he was sure he was going to look more closely at them now.

"So this arranged marriage thing, it was never meant to be permanent?" That was the first question eating away at Jax. Why would they have such an agreement to begin with?

"No. I was to have a son to raise, and she was to have a daughter. That was all we were together for, even if I did fall for Rommy. Her actions make it seem like she never had feelings for me," Wes replied.

Oh, there were feelings, but he was pretty sure they were ones that went along with hate. Any asking about their father would get them a glare they learned to avoid as kids growing up.

"Since your mother didn't teach you about hunters, I'll give you the basics. What you choose to do with your life is your choice, but your mother should have been honest with both of you from the beginning. This might be hard to take in, but all the papers there will back me up."

Jax stared at the man in front of him. His words sounded ominous. His mother kept secrets, as all the hunters did, but Jax never found that a problem. Hunters, in general, were very private people. Even when the hunter families gathered there were secrets. Everyone liked their privacy. Jax agreed with that even if he didn't get much growing up.

"Do you wonder why hunters have greater than normal strength?"

Jax shrugged. Okay, the answer was yes, but he wasn't

about to talk. He had many questions building up in his mind, but Wes was talking and giving out answers freely. He wanted to hear what the guy had to say before asking more and stopping him.

"You never once maybe wondered why they were strong?"

Wes peered at him like he was trying to read his mind. Jax just stared back. Yes, of course, he wondered, and had asked his mother once. It got him a quick rap across his hands that taught him to not ask again.

"Well, hunters' strength comes from what they hunt. The hunters were created to help keep night humans in line. But the problem with that is no normal person could stand toe-to-toe with a night human. Even the lesser night human species are still stronger than a normal human. They wouldn't stand a chance. What hunters needed was to be stronger, quicker, heal faster, and have senses as good as anyone in the night. Hunters needed to be just like their night human prey, but without the need for blood. Hundreds of years ago, the hunter society accidentally came across the answer to this problem when one of the hunter daughters fell in love with a night human. She gave birth to a daughter of her own, and the hunters used that child to start a whole new line of hunters, ones that could stand up to a night human."

Wes paused, and Jax took in what that meant. That hunter that was born was of night human blood, a part night human girl.

"But anyone with night human blood becomes one," Jax pointed out the problem with the story.

"As nature would want it. But somehow the hunters found a way to stop that from happening. From that one child, they changed everything. Before her, hunters had to have dozen of children and train for decades before they could fight the weakest night human. After that, they began a whole new life. They found that all hunters could have two children to keep the entire line going. Haven't you noticed that hunters seem to live longer lives than expected in a profession that should kill them off easily? And have you noticed that everyone has only two children?"

Jax didn't consider living into your forties a long time, but bearing in mind their job was putting their life on the line every day, it was actually longer than it should be. Not to mention the easy healing. That probably saved every hunter multiple times a month.

"So you're saying all hunters have night human blood in them?"

"Correct."

"Which would mean I have night human blood in me?" Jax didn't really want to know the answer, and Wes must have sensed that.

"You are my son, and you asked me before about when I became a night human. That was a very long time ago," Wes answered indirectly. "Vampyres typically don't have children. This makes you very important to me. Have you learned much about the vampyre clan?"

Wes was changing subjects and Jax was thankful for that. He didn't want to think more about what the whole night human hunter thing meant. If that was true, which more than likely it was, he had been lied to his whole life. They had raised him to hate night humans and to believe that they were all evil. He already knew that they weren't all evil. However, to discover he was one of them made it more confusing. Did they look upon their children as half evil also?

"I've had very little training on them. Until I came here, we were told that you guys were pretty much extinct."

Wes grinned now. Jax had a good feeling that was exactly what the man wanted.

"Vampyre don't have children. Unlike other night human clans, the vampyre gene is very dominant. Two vampyre genes will kill a child, so two vampyre parents mean no children. One vampyre gene means the child will kill the mother before they're born, resulting in death of both child and mother. Again, no child is born. It's very rare to find a human capable of carrying a vampyre child. To this day I have only fathered five children, and I have lived a very long time."

Jax wanted to ask about half siblings, but he kept his mouth shut.

"I am the head of the vampyre clan and needed an heir, and that was the only reason I agreed to bond with your mother. She stole you from me knowing perfectly well that I needed you. The hunters protected her—and you—and you were left to grow up knowing nothing of what you truly are. I want to show you the family you should have had, and the first step for that is to meet the rest of the clan. We aren't extinct. I'd love for you to join us tomorrow night. I have much more to explain, but I must get back before sun-up."

Wes walked into the room and placed a card on top of the opened file next to Jax. Jax simply stared at the man. Vampyres couldn't enter a room without an invitation, and his father had done just that. Jax assumed he'd tossed the file into the room before, but now he saw that wasn't true. Wes caught his astonishment.

"You've learned some things about us, and I don't mean to confuse you. Like I said, I'm the head of the clan. The rules that govern my night humans don't apply to me, and neither would they to you as my heir. I don't want you to feel that you have to be one of us. I'm not asking that. I'm asking you to meet the other side of your family before you decide what to do with your life. I know your mother has shown you the hunter side and where your place would be there. I want you to see where your place would be here. With me."

Jax nodded. While he wasn't a fan of agreeing to a meal with a bunch of leeches, he did want to know more. He could see now that his mother had left out so much.

"Wait," Jax called as his father made it back out onto the

patio. Jax remembered Jen. She was a vampyre, but only part time. Was it possible she had hunter blood in her? "Jen …" He wasn't sure what to say.

Wes nodded. "Bring her along. She might want to hear what I have to say, also."

And just like that, Wes was gone. Again, Jax didn't see where and in what direction the man had left. More than anything, Jax wanted to call home and talk to Jade about everything, but he couldn't. His mother had left everything out, and what Jax knew now wouldn't be something his sister could believe. He was going to have to wait for her to come to him with questions, but one thing he did know: he wasn't going back to the hunters. If he truly was half night human, and he did believe Wes when he told him that, then he wouldn't be wanted back there. The hunters all hated night humans as much as his mother. It was hard to believe that she'd had two kids with one, but after sitting with Wes, he could see why. There wasn't much about the man, beyond his disappearing acts, that made him like other night humans.

CHAPTER 9

Jen **threw a** kick and Jax blocked it. She was frustrated, but she was already doing it again without Jax prompting her. She was more determined after their last run in with night humans to get better. She did everything Jax ordered and got back up every time she failed, which was most of the time. While they still had no clue who had come after them and whether or not it was Jax or Jen as the target, Jax agreed that training seemed like the best option. After repeating her kick three more times, Jen plopped to the ground in a heap. Sitting down beside her, Jax stretched his legs as she caught her breath.

"You know, this would be much easier in your night human form," Jax commented.

"And it would be so much easier to drink your blood that way too, but I'm not eager to do that either. Once was enough for me. Your blood tastes different from anything I've ever had before."

"Good different or bad different?"

"Honestly, I thought it would taste bad, but it didn't. So, good different I guess."

Jax shrugged. She wasn't the first night human who suggested that either his or his sister's blood tasted different. Now he had a reason why, but he still hadn't shared that part with Jen. She didn't know he had the folder, and the less she knew, the better. He wasn't completely convinced that the people who attacked them hadn't done so because of what they knew. If she knew anything more, she would be in further danger.

"How much do you know about the vampyre clan?" Jax asked. He was still trying to piece everything together.

"Like what?" Jen asked as she sat up next to him and began stretching also.

"Like, who's in charge, how do they change people and why?"

"Mr. Hunter doesn't know these answers?" Jen teased, reaching for her toes.

"The hunters think the vampyre are extinct since their leader hasn't been seen by a hunter in a few decades, though I never understood why that meant they were extinct."

Jen glanced at the door to the room before turning back to Jax.

"I might have dug around and through my uncle's stuff more than once growing up. I know a bit, but not a whole lot. I discovered he deals with them, but not why or what they do. I have a feeling I don't want to find out, either."

Jax nodded. It would have been okay to ask Wes. He was pretty sure that the man was looking forward to explaining everything, but sometimes Jax wanted to find his own sources and not turn to the guy he felt might still have an agenda.

"From what I found, there's this whole hierarchy in the vampyre clan. There's one guy on top—most people don't talk about him. I haven't heard what his name is. Then there are guys below him, and guys below them. They all cluster into groups, and any new vamp has to be claimed by a group or is killed. The reason people think they've died out is that only the guy on top of everything can create new ones. If someone else tries, they get a blood-hungry monster instead of a person. When the head guy does it, they come back normal. That's what I've found when I went looking, but never once has anyone ever mentioned that the vampyre can have kids, so I have no idea where I come from."

"I've also been taught they can't have kids, but maybe there's something special about you or your mother. You said she was a priestess." Jax might have had a better understanding of that now, but he didn't know what to say to Jen. Jax watched her as she stretched more. She seemed to be completely a day human for the moment. Then again, so did he.

"Yeah, that's what I always figured, but then why didn't she leave me a note or something? There was nothing left behind when she died after making the bracelet. Obviously, she knew what I was and what it meant, yet nothing. No information. Not even initials. At least you have someone to look for. I have nothing."

Jax could understand her frustration. Even just two weeks ago, he'd been in the same boat. He knew nothing. It was ironic that Jax and Jade agreed their code word when danger was coming was their actual, true father's initials, but they didn't know it then. And that was just one more subject to bring up with Wes. Maybe he understood because Jax and Jade never could figure out why Jax could see the future and change it.

"Something is better than nothing, I do agree. It's just sometimes you don't find what you're looking for," Jax added as he stood and offered a hand to Jen.

"We'll figure out your father problem. I think he turned right after your mother left him. That has to be it since you aren't like me. Once we find him and corner him, you can ask all the questions you want." Jen gave Jax a big smile as she took his hand to stand.

Jax had asked questions and gotten a few answers, but there was still so much more. He didn't want to tell Jen he had met Wes already. He needed time to come up with a plan, and he was getting surer that Wes was a slippery night human who stayed hidden. Jen, in all of her searching, didn't know he was the one on top.

They left the training room and began walking toward the parking lot so Jen could head home.

"My uncle asked if you'd like to join us for a late lunch," Jen said as she was looking at her phone, which had just dinged, indicating a text message. "He says he wants to apologize to you about the whole folder incident. He was just following orders. He said that as soon as your father gets back to town, he'll make sure he knows you're here and he'll get you that folder."

Jax looked over at Jen and could tell she was just reading off her phone. There was something fishy going on, and he wasn't sure he wanted to know what it was. They already saw Wes at the party. Was her uncle suggesting Wes was gone again? Jax was planning to have dinner with the man. He sure hoped he wasn't gone again.

"I think I'll just stay here," Jax added.

He really didn't want to get into anything more in town. He had the answer he was looking for, even if it did lead to more questions. He especially didn't want to know what her uncle was doing with night humans.

"Come on. He said he was sorry. He like never does that," Jen added. "He must really feel bad. Come over for food. I'm sure it will be something fancy and good to eat. And you don't have to eat alone, because that's what you were going to do, right? Sit in your room and order room service while you search the Internet for the next place to go for answers? Come over instead, and we can see if we can get anything out of him. He doesn't hold secrets well when he's been drinking. We can booze him up and get some good stuff from him."

Jax still didn't want to go over to her uncle's place. Something about the man seemed off. Maybe it was the whole 'keep him at the office until someone could arrive' game he'd played that made Jax not trust him, but whatever it was, Jax wasn't looking forward to being around him.

Jen stood at the door leading to the garage, pouting. "Please. If you don't want to come over to pry him for answers, just do it to have dinner with me. If you don't, then I have to sit there alone with him and my aunt, pretending we're some happy family."

Jax really wanted to have a good excuse to say no. He could say he needed time to read the folder his father gave him, but that was one secret he planned to keep for now.

And, besides, there was the fact that he had read everything in it already. Jax remembered that they had a dinner date. That would be a good excuse.

"Remember I told you about that thing we need to check out tonight? How about we not do lunch with your uncle and just hang around here until then," Jax suggested.

Jen rolled her eyes as she pushed the door open to the garage and a blast of hot air hit them both.

"How about I go with you tonight, and you can pick me up at my uncle's place and eat before we leave?" Jen negotiated.

Jax could tell this was something she wasn't going to give up on. He shook his head, knowing he was about to do something he didn't really want to do.

"Fine. A quick meal with your uncle and then we can go investigate what I've found." Jax still didn't want to tell her too much and was certain she would be mad about the surprise. Wes was offering answers for both of them, but Jax was keeping it from her for now.

Jax was early when he arrived at the lawyer's house. Either he did far better as a lawyer than his office indicated, or he did something on the side to make good money in order to afford such a luxurious place. Jax pulled through the gates that closed and locked behind him, and he was certain the guy in the booth by the entrance was a night human. It was still daylight, and he suspected the booth was shielded by UV protectant glass—a lot of good he would do if he needed to come out of his protective enclosure—or it was possible he was there for the night watch. The guy nodded to Jax as the gate closed and locked with a clink.

Pulling the car in to park was enough to cause Jen to run outside. He didn't even make it to the door. For only the second time Jax was feeling how young she really was, and maybe more than a little lonely.

"You really did come," she squealed as if she'd doubted he would.

"Yes, and we're going to go later and see what I want to see, right?"

"Of course."

Jen led the way inside the house. Large staircases jutted up both sides of the enormous entryway. The white on white décor was hard to look at, and probably impossible to keep clean. Actually, it was probably the cleanest place he had ever been in, and likely had an army of maids to keep it that way. Hunters weren't the cleanest of professions, but they had to be able to fit in. Jax pretended like he was used to the luxury of the house as Jen's heels clicked on the marble floors, leading the way. He would never be used to money such as this, but he could always pretend. He was actually good at fitting in, even in a place like Jen's uncle's house.

"This way, Mr. Kristian," Jen said in a fake, haughty accent.

"I suppose when you borrow things, they don't notice, do they?" Jax asked, thinking of the car that was likely still a scrap of metal on the side of the road.

"If you're talking about something specific, he actually did notice and sent someone to pick it up already. He's going to have it looked over to see if the brakes were cut or if the lines just went bad. If they were cut, then he can't sue his auto mechanic for doing a bad job with keeping the cars in shape," Jen replied before stopping.

She was standing in front of two large, ornately carved doors. She looked like she might want to bolt as much as Jax did, but she stayed. Instead, she turned to him with a smile.

"Before we go in, please understand that my uncle and aunt have nothing to do with me. They can be a bit overwhelming to deal with, and like to flaunt their money—if you couldn't tell by this place."

Jax smiled. "If you met my mother, you would

understand that I don't hold anyone's guardians over their head. Trust me, parents don't make us into anything. We are completely our own people. With how she was as a mother when I was growing up, I should have turned out to be a serial killer."

Jen laughed. "It couldn't be that bad." She actually thought Jax was kidding. He wasn't.

"You've never met Rommy Kristian, and I promise you never want to." Especially now that he knew she was part night human.

Jen pushed open the doors to the dining room. It was a large room that held a very long table in the center. The table could seat over twenty people, and there was more than ten feet to spare on all sides. The white marble theme was spotted with black and red accents all over the room. The table itself was set for a person at each end and two in the middle, facing each other.

"Welcome to my surreal life," Jen explained as she led the way over to the table.

"We get the middle?" Jax asked when they stopped by one of the chairs. It had a setting at it; white plates, red cups, black napkins, and close to a dozen utensils to eat with. Yeah, it was more than a bit over the top.

Jen made her way around the table and to the other side to face him.

"Of course. The peasants sit in the middle while the king and queen rule," Jen replied in hushed tones. The door to the hallway pushed open again.

This time the same lawyer Jax had met before walked into the room. It was best to describe his movements as strutting the longer Jax watched. The gentleman had to be in his forties or fifties at least, but clearly didn't want to be seen that way. His clothing was all designer, and his tan was more than likely fake, along with his hair color. He walked over to Jax and held out his hand. Jax shook it and wasn't surprised to find he was still just a normal day human. But that didn't mean Jax didn't pick up on the fact that there were night humans all over the place. His senses told him to stay alert.

"Thanks so much for stopping by. My niece said you've been busy. I wish I could help more, and I promise as soon as my client gets into town, I'll call him and get this all sorted out."

Jax nodded absently. He didn't need anything sorted out, and it seemed that Michael Landry didn't know the file was missing, or that his client was in town. All of these details made it seem like Michael Landry was either incompetent or hiding something.

"Where's Aunt Liz?" Jen asked, glancing at the other place setting that no one was claiming.

Michael looked over at Jen as if he just remembered she was still there.

"Liz wasn't feeling well and went to bed early. It's just us." Michael made his way down to one end of the table and sat down. He motioned for Jen and Jax to do the same.

"That's too bad," Jen added. She appeared to be genuinely disappointed.

Jax remained silent and stared at the man. Michael sat down quietly, and Jen held her tongue. He'd been more than talkative the first time they'd met, but something seemed off now. He was still a day human, so that wasn't it, but there was something Jax couldn't put his finger on. Michael seemed nervous ... or was it happy? Something was strange, and Jax had had it with all the strangeness and secrets.

When Michael snapped his fingers, hidden doors on the side of the room opened, and a person rolled a cart through each one. One guy removed the lids of several plates before handing them over to the second person. She skirted around the table and placed salads before each of them. Jen waited as she watched her uncle. He smiled grandly at the two of them and dug right into his food. That seemed to be the cue she was waiting for, because Jen began eating also. Jax ate some of the salad, enough to not seem rude, before he set his fork down. He wasn't really there for the food, and with Jen and Michael busy eating, Jax could just check out the surroundings.

Michael continued his meal slowly, making sure every last ounce of dressing was eaten off his plate. Jen had already finished hers and was waiting also. Jax took his cue from her to not talk as she sat silently. When her uncle was satisfied that he was finished, he snapped his fingers again. The same two people came out and removed the salads before replacing them with soups.

Jax pretended to sip the soup, but the taste was off. Jen didn't seem to notice and ate more than Jax did. Again, they sat and waited for Michael to finish, taking more than twenty minutes to have one cup of soup. Jax had arrived at three, thinking they would be finished eating by four at the latest, but it seemed as if Michael liked his meals to take hours. Jax didn't know how many courses the man planned to serve. He hoped it would be done by the time they had to go over to Wes's place.

They continued to eat the strange meal. Michael ate every last bit in silence, and Jen and Jax nibbled on what they had been given. Watching the older man focus so intently on his food was weird, to say the least, but the amount of time he was taking was getting to Jax. He really didn't want to spend any more time with the man than he had to. By the time dessert came out, the sun was starting to set. Jax didn't like knowing there was a night human at the gate now. It was bad enough he sat there in daylight, but he was effectively harmless until the sun set. Michael didn't seem to care or notice the setting sun from the windows on the far wall of the room.

Two new people pushed carts into the room. His senses told him they were night humans, and Jax gave Jen a kick beneath the table. Jen looked across at him, but there was no way to get her to see what he did. And there was a slight widening of her pupils that concerned him a bit. He was sure they were drinking water and juice, yet she looked like she was starting to get drunk.

The new guys pushed the cart closer to Michael before opening the lid to display an elaborate cake. Michael smiled. He wasn't finished eating. Jax had no clue where the man packed all the calories, but after two hours of eating, maybe it was just spread out nicely. Jax was anxious for the meal to be done, and he was more than ready to suggest they take their dessert to go. The arrival of the night humans was an even better excuse to leave.

Jax reacted too slowly when he realized what was going on. One of the men pulled out a knife that they all assumed was to cut the cake. Instead, it was quickly at Michael's neck.

"Don't move, and he won't get hurt," the night human said in a husky voice. His partner had a knife in her own hand, pointed at both Jax and Jen.

Having someone kidnap her uncle seemed to wake Jen up. She was no longer foggy-looking as she stared at her uncle in shock. How it was shocking to her was beyond Jax. She knew her uncle was knee-deep in night human business and she had to guess the money for their lifestyle came from somewhere.

From the slightly open doors, Jax caught a glance of more people waiting. It was bad enough trying to fight while keeping two day humans safe, but it looked like he had way more to worry about than just taking on two night humans. Jax kept his body straight, and turned his face to the two that held Jen's uncle as he moved his leg slightly enough that he could reach the stake strapped to his leg.

The man pulled roughly at Michael and forced him to stand up. Not that he had much of a choice; there was a blade at his neck. That got most people to move easily. The stocky night human kept Michael glued to him as he pulled the older man around the edge of the room and out the door that Jen and Jax had entered from. He was taking him deeper into the house, which meant there would be a chase once Jax was done with the waiting night humans. Jax was regretting his choice to stay for the meal now.

The girl remained, her knife pointed at Jax as she realized which of them was the real threat. No one was going to take glassy-eyed Jen as a problem.

"You go find your uncle, and I'll deal with this," Jax said. He didn't expect Jen would be able to fight the night human, but he did think she would be able to track them in the house. If he was quick enough with however many of them were waiting, he could catch up with her so she wouldn't have to fight alone.

Jax stood slowly and the night human watched him.

"You seem to think we'll just let her leave," She glared at Jax. "I hate when humans get all cocky. You don't know what you're dealing with."

Jax held a hand out to Jen. She stared at him before reaching across the table to take it, sitting on the table as she did so. Jax smiled. She might not be ready, but he was.

"Well, that's where you're wrong," Jax said, using his free hand to pull back his sleeve and show the mark on his arm. "I know perfectly well what I'm dealing with."

Jax didn't wait for the realization to sink in. She'd come into a situation she hadn't expected, and he could tell. It made for the perfect opportunity for him to get Jen out of her way. Jax gave a tug to Jen's arm and pulled her across the table, splattering food and dishes farther down and onto the floor. Jen was standing beside him, stunned at what he had just done.

"Find them and wait for me," Jax said to her as he pushed her toward the exit.

The stunned night human had rushed back to the door and opened it for her friends to enter. One by one, they came out of the kitchen and into the dining room. They lined up across from him on the other side of the table. Jax didn't need to count to know that there were more night humans in that room with him than he had ever taken on alone before. He had no choice. He needed to keep Jen safe, and to do so it seemed he needed to play the hero and save her uncle. Even though it was very well possible the man deserved what he was being put through. Being a hunter stunk sometimes, but as he reached in his coat and pulled out his gun in one motion, he squeezed off six quick rounds in a row, hitting six different night humans who dropped to the ground. Sometimes being a hero could be fun.

Jax didn't wait to see their shocked faces as he jumped onto the table and pulled out his stakes. No one expected that he would fight back and the unexpected result meant he temporarily had the upper hand. Jax needed to use that to his advantage as he jumped down and shoved a stake into the closest downed night human. He didn't have time to plan as he turned to hit the next one before they realized what he was doing.

After offing two of them, they all seemed to come back to their senses and dragged the other four hurt ones away from him. Jax was standing against four downed night humans—they weren't dead and would be fighting back in no time—and six more ready to pounce. A few of them seemed to be worried about the ones he shot, but the others were baring their teeth. Jax took the moment to reload his gun and was ready for the second round.

"You're really dumb enough to take us all on?" the girl who was still just brandishing a knife asked.

"I don't see it as dumb when two of you are now dead, and four are ready for me to put them out of their misery. See, I switched to wooden-tipped bullets before coming out tonight. I hear that they hurt badly for your kind." Jax gave her a fake sympathy frown before smiling at her. "I'd apologize if you weren't all set on killing me yourselves."

The girl that seemed to be leading them growled. She tossed her knife with quite a force and accuracy, but Jax just twisted and dodged it. He'd been dodging objects thrown by his mother for years and could do it in his sleep. Jax snapped off another round from his gun but missed her as she pulled the guy next to her into the line of fire. The element of surprise was gone, and it was time for the real fight to start. Jax wasn't happy with the odds of five on one, but that wasn't going to make him run away. Hunters never ran away.

The door to the kitchen swung open, and a new person walked in. Jax positioned himself to see the newcomer, but stopped in surprise. It was a new night human, but not entirely new. Jax had seen the same man the day before he left his mother and sister—the night human who had cleaned up the nest for his sister and had ordered him to leave was standing in the doorway.

"Now how in the world is it fair for ten night humans to gang up on one regular old day human?" The man walked into the room with a swagger that indicated he knew what he was doing.

The lead girl vampyre looked at him in confusion. The night human hunter walked closer to Jax.

"He doesn't look tough. Why in the world would there need to be so many of you to take him down?"

Now the hunter was right in Jax's face. He nodded ever so slightly to Jax, and Jax didn't need words to understand. There was something about him that made Jax feel a kinship to him. This man was there to help him. He would have smiled, but the night human hunter looked at Jax's gun and then tilted his head slightly to the left, and Jax understood that as well. As the man turned to his right and moved out of the way, Jax clipped off the last four standing vampyres. They were all on the ground writhing in pain now, except for their leader.

Without another word, the mysterious guy was across the room, taking down the leader of the group while Jax made rounds, staking each of the vampyre on the ground.

"Where's Jen?" the guy asked the vampyre in his arms.

She was bleeding from various cuts. It seemed the hunter didn't use any weapons when he fought.

"She ran off to find her uncle. That leech's partner took off with him," Jax answered for the girl.

The vampyre hunter snapped the neck of the girl in his arms before twisting enough to pop her head right off. Jax was used to violence, but this was a new one. He wasn't sure whether to be disgusted by all the blood, or amazed that a human of any kind could do that.

"Good screw up little hunter boy," the night human hunter said to Jax. "If you couldn't figure this out already, Michael doesn't need saving. These vamps could only enter with his permission, so they'd been here all along."

Jax finally realized what the night human hunter was saying and wanted to smack his own head. That was true, and something he should have realized right at the first moment.

Clapping at the doorway to the hallway drew their attention to the vampyre who had taken Jen. He was walking in with Jen in his arms. Her uncle was beside her, smiling as he clapped.

"Bravo, Beck. Always the one that understands the quickest," Michael said as he looked at the other hunter. "I assume that's why he ordered you to stick around and watch over his son."

Now Jax glanced at the hunter beside him. Did that imply the hunter was making sure he was kept safe? Was it an order from his father?

The hunter, Beck, didn't reply to the provocations. Michael turned back to Jax, who had been holding his gun since he'd reloaded.

"And don't think about shooting my friend here. He's been waiting patiently for my niece to invite you over since you ran away from my office. He's waited a long time to finally find you. Your father kept you well-hidden all these years," Michael explained.

Jax wasn't about to set his gun down.

"Set down the pistol or I slit her throat," Michael added. The knife pressed hard enough against Jen's throat to draw blood.

The hunter beside Jax growled, and Jen looked genuinely scared. She had said her uncle was strange, but he had a feeling she never expected this side of him.

"Why are you doing this to your own niece?" Jax asked, trying to buy time as he thought through all the scenarios that would work the best to get Jen back. He was coming up with a blank and hoped the hunter named Beck beside him had a better plan.

"She isn't my blood. My wife's stupid sister went and had this child. The only reason we've bothered to take care of her all these years is to get the money. Jen came with a wonderful trust fund that has kept us well fed. But she's really no use to me, and I don't care if I kill her. This man here is offering me a lot more than Jen brings in for you and you alone."

Jax didn't know how to respond. Jen looked crushed. While she didn't have tons of love for her aunt and uncle, they were still her family. Jen had nothing else. Jax knew that feeling all too well. His mother and sister left him without much either. They were family, yes, but part of a life he would never be allowed into fully. He was in the same boat as Jen.

The hunter placed his hand on Jax's cut arm.

'Do not give yourself over to that man,' Beck said into Jax's mind.

Jax had known night humans could talk inside each other's minds, and even though he knew now that he was part one, it was still confusing to him how it was possible. How the heck was he supposed to reply to the man? *This wasn't part of night human hunter training.*

He felt the man laugh, but when Jax looked at him, his face was set in a serious mask.

'It is training where I come from. And, basically, I'm making a connection between the cut in my hand and your arm. We need to work together on this. That man wants more than to take and kill you. You're in no shape to stand up to him in this form.'

'What the heck does that mean?' Jax thought, hoping it went across the bond they were forming with their blood.

'That man there is Hector. He is one of your father's five lieutenants. He's one of the oldest and strongest vampyres your father ever made. He won't go down with a few wooden bullets, and he won't just let you stake him. It takes more skill than that to fight a man of his strength, and a little night human blood would help a lot.'

'And I suppose you have that strength?'

'Maybe on my best day, but I wouldn't bet on it. We need to get your sister away from them both. If they figure out who she is, they will kill her, too.'

Jax froze as he looked across the room at Jen. She was his sister. That was why she reminded him so much of Jade. She was blood. And realization set in further. Her mother died hiding away her night human form. She knew who her mother was, which meant they shared the same father, Wes Cunningham.

'She has a night human form?' Beck asked. Obviously, their connection was still there.

'Yes, when she removes the bracelet. Her mother placed a spell on it to keep her night human side away,' Jax explained.

'Then this won't be a problem. Just don't go after Hector. Your father will deal with him.'

Beck returned his attention the two men holding Jen captive.

"We won't be trading Jax for Jen. Sorry, but Jax is too important to just throw away," Beck said as he let go of Jax's arm.

"What?" Jax was ready to fight Beck because of his

words. They were just talking about saving her. Why did he change his mind?

"I see we will have to prove that we don't need her," Michael added, pressing the knife harder against Jen's throat.

Jax didn't care what the night human hunter was doing; he wasn't going to let Jen die for him. Jax moved to go to her side, but Beck grabbed him around the waist, holding his arms down. He was much stronger than Jax expected, and Jax didn't have time to wiggle free.

Michael Landry didn't hesitate to slice his own niece's throat open. Jax let out a growl as he moved to break the hold Beck had on him, but he didn't need to. As he had seen once before, Jen transformed, her bracelet breaking right off her. She turned quicker than her uncle or his friend were expecting, and hit her uncle directly in the face. In an instant, she was across the room aiming to hit Beck also, but he let go of Jax.

"I wasn't going to hurt him," Beck said to the transformed Jen. "Your night human side wouldn't let you die. It doesn't matter what kind of magic your mother used; she wouldn't let you die like that. Now it is time we leave."

The vampyre Beck had called Hector crumpled to the ground beside Jen's uncle before they even had to run away from him. Wes Cunningham stepped over the two bodies.

"Thanks for the call, Beck. I'll take it from here."

Beck gave a short bow to the older vampyre and disappeared from the room.

"Sorry. There was traffic, and I didn't make it in time to take care of this mess. I think it's high time we head back to my place and get everything sorted out."

Jen gave a look to Jax, and he nodded along with Wes. There was much he was going to have to tell her, and more that he needed to ask his own father. Here he had run from one family and now was getting a new one. It was ironic, and still, there was so much left to figure out.

CHAPTER 10

Jax said nothing as the limo they were riding in pulled onto Cunningham estate. It bypassed the ornate house in the front and went deeper back into the property. Jen kept sending Jax glances, but Jax remained silent. He didn't know where to start. In reality, he was just as shocked as she was. Jen was his sister. Wes said he had several children, but he didn't mention when he'd had them, or who they were. Jax hadn't thought any more about it until now.

Wes stared at both Jax and Jen, and also didn't speak. The two new siblings sat side by side in the back of the limo and stared everywhere but at each other and him. Wes just smiled. He had spent a long time dreaming about having more of his children around.

When the car finally stopped, the driver appeared in a flash to open the door. Wes motioned for his two children to exit, but Jax wasn't sure what to make of things. There was a smaller house in front of them that was surrounded by trees. Off to the side was a garage which was attached to the house, but the car stopped outside the front of the place. It seemed too small to be the house of the leader of a whole clan of night humans. Maybe Jax just expected more.

"Thanks, Edward. We won't be going anywhere the rest of tonight," Wes said to the driver, who was bowing to him.

Wes led the way into the front of the house. The shining wood floors and staircase leading to a second floor seemed just a bit less luxurious than the other house. Wes smiled at the stunned-looking Jax.

"As you can tell, I live two lives," Wes explained. "There's the corporate CEO and the normal me. I figured you both would be much more comfortable meeting the real me." Wes led the way past the staircase, through a white cabinet kitchen, and to the family room with plush leather couches. "Would either of you like something to drink? I have some blood in the back of the fridge also if you would prefer." Wes looked at Jen.

Jax almost forgot she was still in her night human form. With the bracelet broken, she couldn't change back. Jax had been sure to collect all the pieces, but he wasn't certain if the magic could be restored if it was.

"I don't drink blood," Jen replied as she walked past Wes into the living room, sitting down on one of the couches.

Jax wasn't sure if he should sit beside her, but he figured the other couch was a better guess. When she found out he knew more about what was going on than he'd let on, it was sure to upset her. He'd seen enough angry night humans to know that sitting next to her could turn out badly. He hoped she wouldn't blame him, but he wasn't sure how she'd react while being her other self. Normal human Jen was bound to forgive him, but since he had only met this side of her once, he wasn't sure night human Jen liked him at all.

Wes joined them in the family room and sat on the third couch, glancing from Jax to Jen.

"First, let me introduce myself. I'm Wes Cunningham, the current head of the vampyre clan."

Jen sucked in her breath. He had saved her, but she hadn't known who he was. Jax didn't need to react because he already knew that and more. She looked at him, and he nodded to her.

"I'm sorry about tonight's events. I didn't want to put either of you two in danger until you were better trained, but things are the way they are. I'm glad that you don't go running off to places unprepared, and if I ever see your mother again, I'll be sure to thank her for training you well." Wes nodded to Jax as he took a sip of the drink in his hand. It was dark red, but Jax had a feeling it wasn't blood. Jen didn't seem to care about the drink at all.

"Is my uncle …" Jen finally spoke.

Jax looked at Wes. He already knew the answer. The man hadn't been moving when they left, and Jax hadn't seen a single breath from him. Jen's hit was on mark, and with her night human strength that had been more than enough to kill him. He wasn't sure she should be told that yet.

"Your uncle chose to support the wrong people," Wes replied, not answering the question. "His choice signed his own death warrant. Anyone in the Hector line will be taken care of, and since your uncle was hoping to be turned by Hector, he's part of that package." Wes shrugged as Jen nodded. She didn't completely understand what Wes was saying, but she would once she thought it all over. Jax would be there for her then.

"Who is Beck?" Jax asked. He had met the night human twice now.

Wes seemed startled by the question, and then smiled as someone came into the room behind them. Jax turned around to find the mysterious night human hunter there.

"Your older brother," Beck answered, sitting on the arm of the couch that Wes was on. "And the one assigned to keep your butt safe. Which, let me tell you, is harder than it looks. I have a job to do, but father here has been constantly worried your mother would get you killed. I was surprised to find it was our little sister that was off getting herself in danger this time. You're normally much sneakier." Beck smiled at Jen.

Wes nodded to the blond-haired guy who didn't appear much older than Jax, but he had a feeling looks were deceptive. Jen just stared in shock. In one day she didn't just lose her family, but also gained a new one. Jax felt the same way, but at least he already knew about Wes.

"Hold on …" Jen held her hand up. "You're saying we're all three related?"

"Four," Wes corrected her. "All three of you are related to me. I'm your father, Jen."

Jen just stared at him. She didn't know what to say, and seemed to be in shock. Jax normally would have laughed to see her at such a loss for words, but it wasn't a laughing matter.

Beck rose, and moved back toward the kitchen. "The witches should be here soon."

"Wait a second," Jen finally found her words. "You're the reason I'm this monster?" She was beginning to get mad, and Jax was happy he chose to sit where he had. She was ready to lash out at anything that got in her way.

And sure enough, Jen launched across the coffee table at Wes. Beck was there before she could reach him and had Jen in the same hold he had used not an hour ago on Jax. Jen screamed and lashed out at Beck, but he didn't move. He was as strong as stone. Beck looked to Wes.

"Take her up to her room. They'll want to work in there anyway," Wes told him. Beck nodded and lifted her right off the ground as she thrashed. "Jax, can you give the lady at the door the beads from the bracelet?"

Jax hadn't heard anyone arrive, but found that Wes was right. There was someone there at the doorway, waiting to be let in. Jax opened the door and handed the middle-aged woman the beads he'd carried in his pocket. She didn't say a word as she walked past Jax and up the staircase where Beck went.

"There's nothing we can do here," Wes told Jax as he put a hand on his shoulder. "We should head over to the main house to get ready for the dinner."

Jax had no idea what the man was talking about, but he got the distinct feeling no one told Wes Cunningham *no*. He gave an order, and you were expected to follow, even if you were his kid. The power radiating off the man made Jax understand disagreeing wasn't the best course, and asking why was also not permitted.

Literally getting ready for dinner wasn't what Jax expected. Wes really meant getting ready; there was a tux waiting for Jax in a room in the larger house they passed on their way in earlier. Jax was in that room with a private bathroom bigger than any bathroom in any of the places he had lived throughout his life. There was a lot of money backing his father, and Jax couldn't help but wonder how much. He had read the file that said he had a trust fund, but there were no numbers attached to it.

As Jax fixed the bowtie around his neck, his father came into the room. He was similarly dressed in a matching tux.

"So, we need to talk a little more before we go to dinner," Wes explained.

Jax had assumed as much. Talking before had ended when Jen got mad.

"Will Jen be okay?"

Wes nodded with a shrug. "As okay as she'll ever be. Her mother didn't like night humans, and didn't figure out that I was one until Jen was born. She tried to get rid of that side of her, but you can't just pull one side out of someone. She created the bracelet with her own life. The witch who came should be able to piece it back together, but Jen will never be what she was meant to be. Her mother took care of that."

"What was she meant to be?" Jax had to ask.

"My child," Wes replied.

That really didn't answer what Jax had asked. He was beginning to see a pattern with Wes. Jax waited for him to explain. Wes walked over to the mirror and looked at himself. He straightened his bow tie.

"You met Beck tonight," Wes said as he turned back to Jax. "He's my child also. What would you call him … a night or a day human?"

That was easy to answer. "He's a night human."

There was a knock at the door. When Wes went over and opened it, Beck was standing on the other side.

"They said it'll take all night, but by morning she should be back under control," Beck told Wes. "They needed to feed her, so I'll have to run out later and get some more blood from the bank."

Wes nodded. "Can you shake your brother's hand for me?"

Beck stepped forward and offered Jax his hand. Jax was unsure what the heck was going on, but he took it and shook it. When Beck let go and left the room, Jax turned to Wes.

"Would you like to change your answer?"

Jax was confused. He was certain both times he met Beck before that he was a night human; he felt the power in him. Even now Jax felt power coming from him, but he was as certain as he was at any other time that Beck wasn't a night human. But how was that possible? It was like Jen's bracelet. Beck seemed to be able to just turn it off.

"That's what a child of a First should be like," Wes replied. "That's what it means to be my child."

Jax walked over to the bed and sat down. Was his father saying that Jax had the ability to turn into a night human by will also, and that Jen should have been able to as well? That made no sense at all. Jax was certain he was just a day human and would only ever just be a day human. There was one or the other. You couldn't be both.

"Explain to me what a First is." Jax was still trying to figure everything out. Nothing made sense now. Everything he had been taught didn't seem to be true.

"A First is exactly what the word means. I am one of the first night humans ever created," Wes answered. "You asked why I became a night human, and I had no answer for you. That's because I needed you to understand more of this world before I told you the truth. I don't know why I became one. It was so long ago; I don't remember."

Jax stared at the man in front of him. He looked like he was in his twenties at the most. Was he telling the truth about how long he had been around?

"How long?"

Wes rubbed his chin. "We are talking over a thousand years, maybe even longer. I don't remember. We didn't keep track of years like we do now when I was made. I truly don't know."

Jax didn't know what to say. That seemed impossible, but there was a lot of impossible going on since he came to New Orleans. He had learned as a hunter to never doubt something was possible, but now he was truly being put to the test.

"There are very few of us left. An especially long life isn't all it's cracked up to be. Most choose death after losing the love of their life. Luckily for me, or rather you, I have yet to find the love of my life."

Jax was still speechless. His young-looking father was so old he didn't remember why he had become a vampyre in the first place, and yet still he hadn't found his true love. Now that one had to be impossible.

"Okay," Jax said, finally sorting through his thoughts, "let's say I believe you. You're some really ancient night human that originates from the beginning of all night humans. What does all of this have to do with me? As we can both see, I'm a human. There might be night human blood in me, but I'm not one. Where do I fit in your night human world? Why did you send Beck to keep me safe?"

Wes laughed. "You seem to forget I was with your mother for three years. I know exactly the type of woman she is, and yes, you needed to be kept safe from her and her demands. You do know your mother took on a chupacabra with her bare hands once and it bit off three of her fingers which had to be reattached, right? She doesn't make the best choices when fighting night humans and would rather win, no matter the cost. Heck, when she was pregnant with both you and Jade, she didn't stop hunting night humans. She had a large nine-month pregnant belly and still chased monsters in the night. She wasn't going to keep you safe. I sent Beck to watch over you."

"Yeah, we can agree Rommy isn't cut out to be a mother. But what does that have to do with me?" Jax was getting sick of his evasion.

"You are my son and my heir," Wes stated bluntly.

Jax still didn't understand. He'd already said Beck was his son and older than Jax. Wouldn't that make Beck his heir? Besides, Beck was the one that could transform into a night human, too. What could Wes want with a day human son?

"And Beck?"

"Is my firstborn son. That doesn't mean he's my heir. Beck's situations makes it impossible for him to be my heir. My heir has to be someone that will grow to be as strong as me. Your mother has the blood of the first hunters. In time, you'll be stronger than Beck. You are my heir."

Jax stared at the man that was his father. How could he know such things? For all Jax knew this guy had spied on him, possibly for his whole life, but Jax was sure they had never met or once stood face-to-face until that party only days ago. There was no way Wes could know that.

"I can see your doubt, but I don't share it. I have a feeling my men don't doubt it, either. That's why Hector targeted you. It's very rare for vampyres to have children. He figured if he took you out, it would kill me and I'd let him take over. He had been planning for a while, but I didn't know he was going to move on you so soon."

"So all those death attempts on us were really on me?" Jax asked. He'd suspected it, but he didn't think it was because of his night human half. He thought it was his hunter half that was being targeted.

"Yes, they were targeting you, but they were being very naïve about it." Wes shrugged.

Jax had a good feeling that the older man had already taken care of things.

"I understand this is all confusing, and there's much to

talk about. There's so much for you to learn, and I wish to teach you, but for your sake, you need to make a choice.

"I truthfully thought you were a girl when you were born, but one of the witches here told me that it wasn't true, and that you were my heir. By the time I went looking for you, your mother had hidden you, and I became depressed. I hid away from the world for years and wallowed in my self-pity. I had a son that wasn't going to be mine. Then I decided that it wasn't fair. I came back into the night human world and sent out people to look for you.

"They found you, and I realized that you weren't mine to claim anymore. All that time I didn't fight for you meant that the hunters trained and surrounded you. I went looking for my other children. I had five including you and your sister. I found Beck and brought him home with me, but as expected, it turned out he wasn't my heir. I found his brother, too, but it was too late for me to take him. He was already under the protection of a night human family. I knew the man that raised him, and he would be safe. I did test him also, and he wasn't my heir. I knew because there were only your two sisters left that you had to be it, but I couldn't get to you. I had to wait until you came to me." Wes walked over to the window and looked outside. He paused while he collected his thoughts.

"What I need you to realize is that you have a decision to make. There are only two places you're safe, with me or with your mother. As my heir, you'll always be a target and not just from within the vampyre clan. Any clan that wants to take me down will go after you. A First only gets one heir. You are mine. To stay safe, you will have to train, learn our ways, and how to be one of us. In time, you will be strong enough to never have to worry about another night human attacking you. I can train you, or your mother can, but alone you won't survive."

Jax wasn't expecting that. He'd gone from being the outcast son who wasn't needed in the hunter world to the heir of his father, a First. That was more than Jax wanted to think about. He was going to need time to understand things, and then to form an opinion about all of it.

"What's the decision?"

Wes rubbed his hands together as he turned back to Jax. "I promise I'll take care of Jen now, so don't let that affect you. I also promise your mother will take care of Jade. It might seem like she doesn't care, but I swear to you that Jade means everything to her. Both of your sisters will be safe."

Again, he wasn't answering the question directly. It was nice to hear that his sisters would be safe, but that didn't tell him what he needed to think about, exactly.

Walking over, Wes placed a hand on each of Jax's shoulders and stared directly in his eyes.

"What you need to choose is whether you want to be my heir or the night human hunter you were raised as. Like I said, there are only two safe places for you. Being something else or being on your own will only get you killed. I'll give you a bit to think about it, but just know I'm not asking you to choose between me and Rommy. This is a choice about what you want. Either you want to stay here and learn how to run our clan, or you want to return to hunting the bad night humans out there. Picking your mother or I is not the question I am asking."

Wes gave his shoulders a squeeze and then walked out of the room. As he paused at the door to close it, he turned back to Jax.

"Dinner will be in an hour. You need to choose by then."

Jax watched the door close as he stood in shock. He was supposed to decide his entire life in one hour? How was that possible? He didn't have all the facts. Even with talking to Wes, Jax still didn't know, or understand, the vampyre. And then there were all the secrets back home. He was sure Jade didn't know about the whole "have a couple kids with a night human" clause part of being a hunter. She would have told him that much. Where did that leave Jax? He'd once dated a hunter, but when she left because she was sick, he never dated again. If he chose to go back there, he was setting himself up to be a second-class citizen who would be expected to raise some other night human's kids. That wasn't much of a future.

Jax shook his head and sat back down on the bed. Pulling out his phone, he stared at the screen. There were still no calls from Jade. He wasn't sure what to do, but he was already dialing her number.

"About time you finally called," Jade said as she answered the line without a single ring. "Mom said I had to let you be, but man it was hard. What stupid situation have you gotten into this time? Where am I going to have to drive now?"

Jax smiled. He thought his Jade was gone, and the sister he grew up with was moving on without him, but here she was.

"I'm not in any trouble. Can't a little brother call because he misses his big sister?"

"Sure, like you miss getting your fingernails ripped off. Really. What are you into now? Did you go to visit Whitney and Sam? I heard his band was going on tour soon. I figured you ran away to join them, and I really don't blame you."

Now that sounded like fun. But it hadn't been an option then, and according to his father, it wasn't an option now. Too bad, though, because he was pretty sure Sam would let him join their band. Sam was one of those rare good night humans that Jax had met and befriended through Sam's girlfriend, Whitney. Jax was pretty sure he could always go live with them, but now that he knew the truth Jax didn't want to bring any of his drama or assassins near his friends. He didn't want to bring them near his sister, either.

"Aw, you miss me so much, you're speechless," Jade said in a sickly-sweet voice.

"I miss beating you at the shooting range," Jax joked

back.

Jade booed him over the phone before he heard their mother in the background.

"Rommy's wondering when you're heading home," Jade finally said.

"Not sure yet," Jax replied. "I still have some more stuff to sort out."

Jade relayed the message to their mother. Silence followed, and then a door slamming.

"I will say I'm surprised that she got mad at that. When you left she was mad for like ten minutes and then just pretended like you were on a mission," Jade explained. "I don't know why she's reacting now. I'm the one who's been constantly worried to the point that she forbade me from calling you. She said you would return when you were ready. So, seriously. Rommy's not here. When are you coming back?"

"I don't know if I am," Jax replied honestly. As big of a pain in the butt as Jade could be, she was still his sister. She deserved the truth, or as much as he could tell her. "Don't tell Mom, but I went looking for our father, and I found him. He asked me to stay."

Now there was a string of curse words on the other end of the line. Finally, she got it all out and came back.

"You found him?"

"Yes, and it turns out he didn't leave us. Mom left him."

Jade started laughing. "Yeah, I always thought her version sounded wrong for some reason. Well, I'm happy you found him, and maybe that's where you need to be for now. I'd really like you back."

"To boss around," Jax interjected.

"To be my brother. But I get it. There aren't many guys around here. I have no idea how I'm supposed to date a hunter's son and get married. I get why many of the girls stay single."

Jax wasn't going to explain what he knew about that, and

he was happy she couldn't see his face.

"Thanks, sis," Jax said. He really meant it. No matter if Wes said she'd be okay, Jax still wanted to look after her. She was all he'd had growing up, and he didn't want to be without her. He was also afraid she'd do something stupid thinking she was a great hunter and not a newbie, and he felt as though he needed to be there to keep her safe. Her telling him to stay was what he needed to be free enough to make that choice. If she had begged him to come home, his choice would have been made for him. But now he could create his own future.

"No prob, little bro. Now that you called me, maybe Mom won't forbid me from calling you when I want to."

"Any time," he replied. "Stay safe and don't let Rommy drive you nuts."

Jade laughed. "You, too."

Jax hung up. He had thought talking to her would make his decision for him. He was wrong. He now had to make a choice.

Jax walked over to the window and stared outside. He hadn't noticed the room had a perfect view of the city—showcasing the twinkling lights of a place that didn't sleep. He had a feeling it was a night human's paradise; the French Quarter full of people to feed on who would be too drunk to remember. That was the hardest part of the decision. Everything he had been taught to believe was based on rejecting the very thing asking him to stay. Could he be happy living with night humans?

A knock at the door meant it was time. Jax's hour was up, and he still wasn't certain what to do. When he opened the door, Henry Lawrence stood on the other side waiting for him.

"Your father asked me to fetch you," Henry said as he

pushed up his glasses.

Jax just shook his head. With night human blood running through him, Henry should have had perfect vision. The glasses made no sense. Jax followed behind him as he led the way down the hallway.

"Why did you become a night human?" Jax asked as they walked.

Henry stopped in his tracks. "I was dying. I had two options: die or drink blood for the rest of my life. It wasn't that hard of a choice."

Jax stared at him. Henry was still in the body of a middle-aged man and had hair that was graying. The night human blood didn't turn him young, it just prolonged his life. Jax didn't understand why he would want to live forever, especially since he had his wife and kids. What made him give all that up?

"I thought I could have it all," Henry continued explaining. "I chose to become this, but it was the coward's way out. I should have faced my fate instead of trying to change what I really was."

"If you could do it over …"

"I'd let myself die," Henry answered. "I didn't think about what I was doing. Not that life here is bad. In fact, I was pleasantly surprised to find that your father runs a really good clan. The vampyre keep to themselves. They don't go on murderous sprees like other night humans, and we aren't in any clan wars over land or anything. Your father knows what he's doing, and is—in my opinion—one of the good guys. I just didn't think through my choice before I made it. I tried to change my fate."

Jax nodded as Henry began to move again. That was the part Jax was having trouble with. He didn't know what his fate was supposed to be. Here he was half night human, half hunter, but neither place felt like home. He wished there was a third option, even if it were just running away, but his father was telling the truth. There wasn't anywhere to go.

Henry stopped at the stairs and bowed. Beck was there waiting.

"I'll leave him to you," Henry told Beck.

Beck nodded. "I have a feeling, little brother, that we need to talk," he said as he led the way downstairs. Instead of heading into the house, he walked them outside.

Hearing "little brother" from a man he had met twice felt odd.

"You know, I have another younger brother out there. We grew up together. I don't ever get to see him again, but he's out there. I've heard he's married and has a family," Beck told him. "We have a niece." Beck tucked his hands in the pockets of his jeans and walked them around the side of the house. It was dark out, but with the inside lit up, Jax could see inside perfectly.

"Our father needs you," Beck continued. "I wasn't the heir, and neither was my brother. He only gets one chance at this, and I know he made it seem like you have a choice, but you don't. If you go back to the hunters, they will never let you return. You'll be a hunter forever, and the vampyre clan will die when he does."

Jax still wasn't sure that was completely bad. He'd been attacked more than once by vampyres since he had arrived. However, Henry made Jax remember that there were good in the night human clans, too … but that didn't mean Jax wanted to save an entire clan. And he wasn't sure he wanted to be an heir, whatever that meant.

Looking inside, Jax could see that his father was seated at the head of the table. No one spoke to him, but conversed with their neighbors instead. Wes sat and watched the night humans around him, but he wasn't part of it. He was separate.

"I get that you get to choose between two options that you don't want, either, but that's life, little brother. We don't always get the cards we want. I wanted to grow up with my mother and stepfather. I wanted to see my little brother grow up. I didn't want to be killed before I was legally an adult and turn into a night human, but that was my fate. The question is, what's yours?"

Jax had been wondering that for over an hour. It would have been nice if everything could be laid out and decided for him. In his mind, the choice was halfway to impossible.

"Why do you care so much?"

"Because Father saved me. He brought me back from the dead. He awoke the night human in me that allowed me to join the hunters to keep what happened to my family from happening to anyone else. He freed me from the life that I lost and gave me a new one. He's offering the same to you, if you have the courage to take it."

"And what if I don't want to be a night human?" That was the one thought that Jax kept getting stuck on.

Beck laughed. The serious night human hunter actually laughed.

"Little brother. It isn't the choice of being a night human or not. No matter what you chose, you'll always be one of those. It's a choice of whether you learn how to live with it, or allow yourself to continue to hate it."

Beck walked up to the glass door and opened it. Wes rose from his seat, but he didn't smile. He looked from Beck to Jax, who stood outside the door and gazed into the house. There was a large table laid out at which sat more than fifty people. No one seemed to notice that Beck had entered, but all eyes were glued on Wes. They seemed in awe of the man studying Jax.

'Have you made a choice?' Wes asked inside Jax's head.

Yet another thing Jax was going to have to ask about, because—with more than ten feet between them—Jax had no clue how the old vampyre was in his head. Jax gave one curt nod to his father.

'If you wish to stay, join me for a drink. If you wish to leave, then leave.'

Wes was getting right to the point. He wasn't going to

beg Jax to stay, even if Beck seemed to think the older night human needed him. Wes was leaving the decision entirely up to Jax.

Jax weighed his options one last time. In his almost eighteen years alive, he was making the biggest decision he would ever have to make. If he chose to join Wes, it would change everything. Life as he knew it would be done. There would be no going back. But that didn't mean things weren't already changing. Jax knew the truth now. He couldn't go back to the hunters and pretend otherwise.

When Jax stepped over the threshold, it was as if Wes let out a big breath Jax didn't realize he was holding. He held up a glass, and Jax accepted it.

"I'd like to welcome you all tonight to our dinner," Wes said with happiness in his voice. "I wish to present to you, my heir. My son, Jaxton."

All eyes turned to Jax, standing next to his father.

"To Jaxton!" the people around the table all cheered as they lifted up their glasses in salute.

"To Jaxton," Wes said quietly as Jax tipped back the glass to take a sip of whatever his father had handed him.

Fire spread throughout his body as Jax turned to his father. The older night human smiled. Jax almost would have started swearing over making a terrible decision if the people around him weren't all staring at him in awe. As quickly as the pain made its way through him, it subsided, and Jax felt fine again. In fact, he felt more than fine. He felt like he was re-energized and could run a marathon.

"Welcome to the family, Son," Wes said as he reached forward and pulled Jax to his side. "My son. My heir."

Everyone around them cheered. Jax had no idea what he had drunk, or why he felt so good, but he did know everything was changing. He could feel it not just inside himself, but all around him. Maybe that was fate telling him he had made the right choice. He had been searching for his destiny and found it. He was finally home.

People around him raised their glasses and cheered loudly for Jax. He couldn't help the smile forming on his lips. He turned to the man right next to him and found Henry Lawrence. The older man smiled, too. Jax nodded before catching his own reflection in the man's glasses. A mark was across his forehead. He turned back to his father. Wes smiled at him, revealing pointy fangs as he sipped the glass of red liquid that looked quite similar to Jax's glass. In fact, it smelled similar, also. Jax noticed it then, the mark across his father's forehead as he stood there in his night human form. It was exactly like his. Jax was a night human. A vampyre.

ACKNOWLEDGEMENTS

To you, the reader. <u>Thank You</u> for taking the time to read this story. If you liked it, please leave a review on your favorite online bookseller (or all of them!) and connect with me social media. The greatest help you can do to keep a writer going is to support them by spreading the word about their books.

Also I would like to thank my editors and cover designers. A good editor is essential to getting the story correct (and in my case- several). Thank you so much, Kathie at Kat's Eye Editing, Melissa at There for You Editing, and Ashton Brammer. They work so hard to get you guys the best book. A thank-you to my *AMAZING* cover artist Jessica for such a pretty cover- doesn't she do great work!! I'm beyond fortunate to have found these wonderful professionals to work with.

I'd also like to thank my hubby – who is the only reason I actually even published. He gives me time when I need it to work on my stories. He encourages me to keep going each and every day on this adventure. And he does all the behind-the-scenes effort to make this work. This would be so much harder without his help. So thank you, B. for pushing me off the deep end (or the cliff as I see it sometimes). And a great big thanks to my little munchkins who keep me going from before the sun comes up 'til long after it sets. Love you AK, KB, and EM.

<u>Thank you so much for taking the time to read my novel!!</u>

ABOUT B. KRISTIN McMICHAEL

Originally from Wisconsin, B. Kristin currently resides in Ohio with her husband, three small children, and three cats. A former cell biologist, she now does the mom thing of chasing kids, baking cookies, and playing outside while writing full time. She is a fan of all YA/NA fantasy and science fiction. Find her at www.bkristinmcmichael.com and Twitter, Facebook, Instagram, and Goodreads under B. Kristin McMichael.

BOOKS BY B KRISTIN MCMICHAEL

- To Stand Beside Her

Chalcedony Chronicles

- Carnelian
- Chrysoprase
- Aventurine
- Chrysocolla

The Night Human World series:

The Blue Eyes Trilogy (series 1)

- The Legend of the Blue Eyes
- Becoming a Legend
- Winning the Legend

The Day Human Trilogy (series 2)

- The Day Human Prince
- The Day Human King
- The Day Human Way

The Skinwalkers Witchling Trilogy (series 3)

- The Witchling's Apprentice
- The Wendigo Witchling
- The Witchling Seer

The Merworld Trilogy (series 4)

- Waves and Secrets
- Water and Blood
- Songs and Fins
- Scales and Legends

The Hunter Trilogy (series 5)

- The Night Human Hunter
- The Night Human Heir